Also by Royce Buckingham:

Demonkeeper

Goblins! An UnderEarth Adventure

the dead boys

Royce Buckingham

G. P. PUTNAM'S SONS

An Imprint of Penguin Group (USA) Inc.

G. P. PUTNAM'S SONS

A division of Penguin Young Readers Group. Published by The Penguin Group. Penguin Group (USA) Inc., 375 Hudson Street, New York, NY 10014, U.S.A. Penguin Group (Canada), 90 Eglinton Avenue East, Suite 700, Toronto, Ontario M4P 2Y3, Canada (a division of Pearson Penguin Canada Inc.). Penguin Books Ltd, 80 Strand, London WC2R 0RL, England. Penguin Ireland, 25 St. Stephen's Green, Dublin 2, Ireland (a division of Penguin Books Ltd.). Penguin Group (Australia), 250 Camberwell Road, Camberwell, Victoria 3124, Australia (a division of Pearson Australia Group Pty Ltd). Penguin Books India Pvt Ltd, 11 Community Centre, Panchsheel Park, New Delhi—110 017, India. Penguin Group (NZ), 67 Apollo Drive, Rosedale, North Shore 0632, New Zealand (a division of Pearson New Zealand Ltd). Penguin Books (South Africa) (Pty) Ltd, 24 Sturdee Avenue, Rosebank, Johannesburg 2196, South Africa. Penguin Books Ltd, Registered Offices: 80 Strand, London WC2R 0RL, England.

Design by Richard Amari.
Text set in Goudy Old Style.

Library of Congress Cataloging-in-Publication Data
Buckingham, Royce. The dead boys / Royce Buckingham. p. cm. Summary: Timid twelve-year-old Teddy Mathews and his mother move to a small, remote desert town in eastern Washington, where the tree next door, mutated by nuclear waste, eats children and the friends Teddy makes turn out to be dead. [1. Ghosts—Fiction. 2. Supernatural—Fiction. 3. Trees—Fiction. 4. Missing persons—Fiction. 5. Moving, Household—Fiction. 6. Washington (State)—Fiction. 7. Horror stories.] I. Title. PZ7.B879857Ded 2010 [Fic]—dc22 2010002850

ISBN 978-0-399-25222-8
7 9 10 8 6

ACKNOWLEDGMENTS

I'd like to thank my editor, John Rudolph, who cut my first draft in half and believed I could fix it. Thanks, John, I think we've found the story's place.

I'd also like to thank my friend Eric Richey, who has a good idea every once in a while.

Finally, I'd like to thank the federal government for dumping nuclear waste in my water until I was five years old, and without whom the mutant kid-eating tree in my backyard never would have grown . . .

Royce

PROLOGUE

In its early years, the sycamore tree stretched its branches up toward the light, reaching for the desert sun and its life-giving energy. Beneath the ground, it groped for scarce water and nutrients. Its roots ran far and deep through the dry sand to find what it needed, and when they finally reached the huge Columbia River nearby, it drank heartily.

But it found something else in the water it hadn't expected—warm energy similar to the kind it drew from the sun. The tree soaked up the new radiation directly into its porous wood. It couldn't know that the energy came from the Hanford nuclear plant upriver.

Over time, the tree changed. It grew unnaturally large above the ground and even larger underneath. Before, it had struggled in the arid desert, but now it thrived on the strange nourishment it had discovered, and it grew hungry for more.

Then one day, a twelve-year-old boy climbed the tree's limbs to hide in the large hollow of its trunk. The ravenous tree felt his youthful energy, and it wanted that too.

The boy would not go down while his angry father roamed the yard, screaming for him to come back and take his medicine. As the boy sat tucked away in the tree, the desert heat overcame him. He began to grow weak, dehydrated, and he fainted.

Before long, the boy was dying. But the tree caught him in the place between life and death. It found that it could absorb the boy's vitality as it slowly leaked from his body. It sheltered him and would not let his spark wink out completely, for the boy's life force proved to be as potent as the sun, the earth, and the waterborne radiation. In fact, it was the most powerful energy source of all.

Years later, however, when the boy's energy was almost fully sapped, the tree began to grow hungry again. . . .

CHAPTER 1

Teddy Matthews rolled down the car window, and a wall of hot air blasted him as though he'd just yanked open an oven. He rolled it back up and adjusted the air conditioner to blow directly on his face.

"It must be a zillion degrees out there," he said.

"Welcome to the desert," his mother replied with the smile she wore when she was trying to make unpleasant things seem not so bad. It was the same smile she'd used when she first told him they were "relocating" to the middle of nowhere and leaving all his friends behind.

He shifted his feet atop a moving box on the floorboards

and stared out at the tan expanse of sand as his mom drove them toward their new home in Richland, Washington.

"I thought that Washington was the Evergreen State," Teddy said.

"That's the west side of the state," his mom said. "They don't get much rain over here in southeastern Washington. Almost all of the water comes from the Columbia River."

"Isn't that where the nuclear plant dumps its waste?"

"Don't be silly," she replied. "They stopped doing that years ago. The town is completely safe now."

She was a lab chemist and had a job lined up at the plant, so Teddy didn't argue about the nuclear stuff. Instead he said, "Sure, completely safe, except for the scorpions."

"Whose venom is no worse than a bee sting," his mother assured him.

"What about rattlesnakes?" he tried.

"They keep to dark holes mostly, and they're more scared of us than we are of them."

"Oh, I doubt that very much," Teddy said.

"It's the black widow spiders that actually get into the houses." She winked at him. "Watch out for those."

Teddy shuddered. "You know, Mom, most people stay far away from creepy, poisonous things. They don't move to the desert to live among them."

"C'mon," his mother prodded playfully. "Once we get there, you just need to find your place. Don't worry. I'm sure there will be lots of kids for you to meet."

Teddy sighed—he couldn't help but worry. He was about to become the new kid in a strange town for the first time in his life.

They turned onto the Vernita Bridge, which crossed over the Columbia River. It was strange to see a river in the middle of the desert, especially the biggest river in the Pacific Northwest. It bullied its way through the dry landscape like a giant serpent swallowing up the sand and everything else in its path.

Fifty miles down the river, they came to Richland.

The highway into town took them past a dump where the heat was busily decomposing the stinky garbage, then a gated cemetery, which didn't look very restful sitting beside the noisy road, and finally a run-down trailer park with a wooden sign the relentless sun had bleached almost white.

The faded letters read DESERT OASIS! But nothing about the trailer park, or the town for that matter, looked like an oasis to Teddy.

Richland wasn't large. Five more minutes, and they were at their new house.

"So this is the place the government is renting for us," his mom declared as they stepped out of the car. "Two thousand square feet and new brown carpet. Great, huh?"

Teddy surveyed the block. His new home was a two-story split-level with an attached garage and a huge picture window in front. It was nearly identical to the other houses up and down the street. They were all beige with two stories, and each had the same big window beside the front door. The only difference seemed to be the shade of beige and which side of the house the garage was on.

The street was empty in the midday heat, which the radio had said was over one hundred degrees. Teddy supposed there might be other kids in the neighborhood, but there would be no school to help him meet them for another month. Until then, he was on his own.

To the left of his house, a slightly lighter beige house boasted a bright green lawn, and, just as Teddy began to wonder how it stayed so healthy, an automatic sprinkler popped up and sprayed water across his shoes.

"Nice," he mumbled, scrambling backward.

On the other side of his yard stood the only unique house on the street. The place was big, square, and looked much older. Its chimney was missing bricks, and its small windows were so dirty they'd turned brown. Rotten wood awnings hung out over them like droopy eyelids. Desert sand was piled up against the front door, making the place look neglected and lonely.

As Teddy stared at the decrepit house, a huge shadow fell across his face. He looked up. A massive, twisted sycamore tree stood in the old house's yard, and its leafy branches blocked out the sun, darkening both the dingy house next door and Teddy's new home. Despite the heat of the day, Teddy felt a shiver run down his spine.

While his mother searched for the key to their own house, Teddy snuck around the fence for a closer look at the abandoned place. Dead grass and dry weeds crinkled beneath his feet, while the tree hovering over the yard seemed in perfect health. It was as though the giant thing was sucking the life from all the plants below, and the lawn was a graveyard of the dried yellow husks of its victims.

He crossed the yard to the porch, where the floorboards were cracked and split. The paint had almost completely peeled off the walls of the home, but it looked as though, in a happier time, it too might have been painted beige. One of the dirty windows was ajar. It would be easy to sneak inside, and Teddy had a sudden, creeping feeling that the old place *wanted* someone to visit.

The porch creaked, making Teddy jump. To his surprise, he found himself standing smack in the center of the splintered old thing. He hadn't realized he'd even mounted the steps. Now he was within arm's reach of the doorknob.

Teddy backed away from the old house, a little spooked that he'd been so drawn to its rickety porch. He felt for the steps behind him with his foot, but when he eased down off the porch, his shoe caught on something. As he fell, he made a grab for the rail, but his hand glanced off and dragged across a loose nail instead. In the hot sun, the rusty metal felt strangely cold slicing into his wrist.

Teddy landed flat on his back in the tall, dead weeds beneath the sycamore. The tree's green leaves seemed to turn away from the sun and look down at him. A large root had caught his shoe, and a few drops of blood from his arm dribbled onto the twisted wood, where they quickly soaked in.

Teddy's head swam—it was hot, and the sight of even a little blood had always made him woozy.

A car horn sounded nearby, and the sudden noise brought him back to his senses. Teddy shook his head clear, jumped up, and hustled back to his own porch as a mail carrier stomped up his walk.

"You live here?" she asked.

Teddy nodded, and she thrust a pile of mail wrapped with a rubber band at him.

"Here's a week's worth," she said. "Been waiting for you to move in." She nodded at the old house. "Whatcha doing hanging around that nasty place?"

"Nothing?" Teddy replied.

"A kid disappeared there, you know." Without any further explanation, she marched back down the walkway and drove off.

Nope, he thought. *I did not know that.*

Teddy stuffed his hand in his pocket. It wasn't a big cut, and he didn't want to explain what happened to his mom.

He slunk around the house to the back door to avoid her, but there she stood in the kitchen, stuffing Tupperware into cupboards.

"Soooo? How do you like it?" she asked.

"It's, uhh . . . great," Teddy lied. "Almost like a normal town."

"Good!" She nodded, pushing a mixing bowl into a full cabinet and slamming the door closed before it could fall back out. "I got you a Hide-a-Key to stick out in the yard so you don't have to carry a key with you when you leave."

"Leave?"

"You know, to explore the neighborhood and make some friends. I'm hoping with a new start you might come out of your shell a little."

"I dunno, Mom," Teddy said. "I kinda like my shell. It's safe in here."

"Out," she said, friendly but firm. "And don't come back until you've met some other kids."

CHAPTER 2

Teddy pedaled his bike down the street with a bandage on his wrist and his face greased with sunscreen to ward off the desert sun's radiation. He rode past a few cul-de-sacs lined with more houses that looked just like his, each with a pop-up sprinkler system and a green lawn. None were like the old house with the dead yard next door.

Less than a mile from his home, he saw a sign for Leslie Groves Park. A park seemed like a nice place to explore, but when he crested a small hill he saw that the "park" was little more than a strip of ragged yellow scrub brush that began where the tidy green lawns ended.

Beyond the scrub brush, the Columbia River cut a vast swath through the sand-and-tumbleweed terrain. It split into two huge channels around a small gravel island. Each channel was more than a football field wide, and the island itself was bare and only about three feet high. It was covered with squawking white seagulls, even though Richland was hundreds of miles from the ocean, in the middle of the desert.

Teddy almost rode away, but then he noticed a boy standing on the near shore flinging rocks toward the gulls. The kid was chubby, about his own age, and wearing very odd bell-bottom pants.

For a few minutes, Teddy just stood straddling his bike and watched the kid, waiting for a good opportunity to say something. Then, without thinking, he rolled forward, and his bike thumped off the end of the sidewalk into the dirt. The boy heard the noise and whirled around, startled. Teddy was now too close *not* to say something.

"Hey bro." Teddy offered.

The boy glared at Teddy. "What do you mean, 'bro'?"

"Uh, I mean, hi," Teddy clarified.

"Oh. Hi." The boy seemed to relax. "What's wrong with your face?"

"Nothing," Teddy replied, then he remembered the shiny layer of sunscreen. "Oh, this? It's Suntastic eighty. It protects against the sun."

"You need protection to go out?"

"Sort of," Teddy said. He pointed across the water, hoping to change the subject. "So, uh, are you trying to hit those birds?"

"Naw. They're too far away, and I don't have an arm that good," the boy explained. "Besides, that would be mean. But I heard that if you can splash one close to the flock, they'll all fly off at once like a big white blanket, and that would be cool to see."

Another awkward moment of silence made Teddy wonder if he should make up an excuse to leave. But his mom had been very clear about trying to meet some kids, so Teddy dismounted and found a large stick. He chucked it into the water.

"That current looks strong," he said.

"Yup."

Submerged snags just below the surface held the stick up for a moment, then the current shook it loose and swept it downstream. Teddy picked up a rock and nailed the stick with a giant splash before it could get away.

The boy gave him two thumbs up. "Ayyy! Nice one. You got an arm like Pete Rose." He stepped forward and held out a pudgy hand, palm up. "Give me some skin."

"Thanks," Teddy said, slapping his hand. "I'm Teddy."

"Teddy Bear!"

"No, just Teddy," Teddy said, not sure if the boy was somehow making fun of him. "What's your name?"

"Albert." The boy smiled a big, open grin that made his eyes squinch up. "I know. It's not a cool name either, but it'll be Big Al as soon as I'm old enough to drive a forklift and get a union job out in the area, eh, Ted?"

"The area?"

"You know, the site." Teddy still wasn't sure what he was talking about. "The Hanford nuclear plant? Ring a bell?"

"Oh, right," Teddy said quickly.

"You're not from here, huh?"

"Nope," Teddy confirmed. "Just biked in from out of town."

"Funny. You should be a comedian."

"Naw, I'm studying to be a video game tester."

Albert gasped. "They have that now? Oh, man, that would be the best job in the world! I love Space Invaders." He held his thick arms to his sides and rotated them up and down at the elbows while making electronic game noises. "Boomp-boomp-boomp-boomp-wee-wee-wee-wee-woop!"

Teddy laughed. "Yeah. I guess that's sorta retro cool."

Albert picked up another stick and a handful of rocks. "Prepare to fire!" he barked. Then he tossed the stick in the water and began hurling the rocks.

Teddy filled his pocket with round stones, and together they peppered the floating wood, challenging each other to see who could hit it the most times before the river spirited it away.

They repeated the routine twice more while Albert quoted lines from the original *Star Wars* movie and celebrated each of Teddy's hits with an enthusiastic whoop. He added a brief victory dance whenever he nailed a stick himself, which was less often.

It was fun, and Teddy was just beginning to think he might have met a friend on his first try, when Albert suddenly fell silent and straightened up, alert, his head rotating back and forth as he scanned the shore. He looked, Teddy thought, like a gopher sensing trouble.

"Uh-oh!" Albert said. "It's Henry Mulligan." He threw himself flat behind a tumbleweed next to the riverbank. "Stay calm. Don't freak out," he said, waving for Teddy to join him on the ground.

"Who?" Teddy looked around, wondering why Albert was freaking out. He didn't see anybody, but Albert was waving so frantically that he crouched low just in case.

"You really aren't from here," Albert said. "Henry Mulligan! He's fourteen and carries a knife this big." Albert held his hands six inches apart to demonstrate its size.

Teddy cringed—he didn't like knives, or the blood they could produce.

"He was hanging out behind the Uptown Theater today with his smoking buddies," Albert blustered. "They must have seen me!"

"Maybe they just *act* tough."

"No way. Henry's like the Darth Vader of junior high. He once made a kid eat boogers."

"Uh . . . some kids do that anyway."

"*Henry's* boogers—at knifepoint. C'mon, man, we gotta get out of here!"

Teddy looked around again. "I don't see anyone. How do you know he's coming?"

"He always does."

Teddy wasn't sure what that meant, and Albert didn't explain.

"Into the river," Albert ordered. "He won't follow us there, and we can float away. We'll meet at the Bookworm if we get split up."

Teddy wasn't convinced swimming for it was the best plan, though Albert seemed insistent.

"What's the Bookworm?" he asked.

"The bookstore on George Washington Way," Albert sputtered, exasperated. "It's behind Malley's Pharmacy. Now get in the water!"

"Y'know, if he's walking, I think we can outrun him on our bikes," Teddy said.

"Negatory. C'mon!" Albert beckoned from the river's edge.

Just then, an older kid sauntered over the hill. He was tall and had stringy hair. His mouth was drawn into what looked like a permanent sneer, acne was ravaging his face, and he wore a sleeveless muscle shirt.

"Hey, looky there!" Henry Mulligan announced. "Two snot-eaters for the price of one!" He hawked up a huge, phlegmy mouthful of spit.

Albert began to shake, and Teddy wondered if the kid from the story who ate boogers had been Albert himself.

"Okay, buddy," Teddy said, putting a hand on the chubby boy's shoulder, "maybe if we stick together he won't try anything."

"Buddy?" Albert brightened. "You mean that? You'd stick up for me?" He grabbed Teddy's arm tightly and whispered, "Hey, listen, I'm sorry for dragging you into all this. This is your chance. Forget you saw me, bike away, and don't look back."

Teddy thought about it. It sounded like good advice, but abandoning the fat kid to a bully seemed a bad start to his first potential friendship. So he didn't run.

To his dismay, two more teens came over the hill behind Henry. They wore black rock-concert T-shirts, had long hair like Henry, and looked very much like they might also carry knives.

"C'mon," Teddy urged. "To the bikes!" He darted to his own bicycle.

Unfortunately, Albert was not so swift, and it was hard for him to run in bell-bottom pants. The chubby boy only made it a few yards before he stepped on his own pant leg and fell face-first into the dirt.

"He's down!" Henry crowed, well ahead of the other two boys. Teddy saw Henry's green eyes zero in on Albert, who lay curled on the bank. "We got him!"

"You swim for it," Teddy said as Albert groaned and crawled for the river. "I'll see you at the Bookworm!"

As Teddy hauled his bike up off the ground, he saw that Albert wasn't going to make it in time. At the same moment, he realized that he still had some rocks in his pocket. He pulled out one of the round stones, cocked his arm, and hurled it in Henry's direction, hoping to make the charging bully stop or even just duck for cover.

To Teddy's horror, Henry didn't stop or duck. He kept coming. And with a sickening *thud*, the rock hit him above the left eye.

Henry staggered behind a yellow patch of scrub brush, clutching his head. "You're a dead man!" he yelled, and he waved to his buddies, motioning for them to hurry. But they hesitated to make sure no more rocks were coming.

While the magnitude of what he'd just done sank in for Teddy, Albert pushed himself out into the water. Seeing that Albert had escaped, Teddy took off on his bike in the other direction, pedaling like mad.

Once he was twenty yards up the street, Teddy risked a look over his shoulder. Henry had emerged from the brush to chuck rocks at Albert, but it looked as though Albert had gotten the head start he needed; he was already almost out of range and floating down the river.

As the powerful current dragged Albert away, Teddy waved good-bye to his first potential friend. He hoped that Albert could swim well enough to flounder ashore downstream. Then he pedaled off to find the Bookworm.

Teddy biked hard for five blocks until he hit the town's main drag, George Washington Way.

He found Malley's Pharmacy and circled around the back twice, but there was no sign of the Bookworm—just an empty storefront. He sat on his bike and waited for ten minutes, but Albert didn't show. So Teddy went inside Malley's to ask where the Bookworm was.

The silver cowbell hanging on the door of Malley's clanged when Teddy walked in. It was an old shop with crowded shelves and a tiny pharmacy counter.

"Help ya, sweetie?" asked an equally tiny woman at the counter, whose nametag read JUDY.

"I'm looking for the Bookworm," Teddy said. "It's supposed to be around here."

Judy wrinkled her forehead. "The Bookworm moved," she said.

"But my friend said it was here," Teddy insisted.

"Do you see it here?"

"No. I guess not."

"Sorry, it moved across town to the Parkway *years* ago. Anything from this decade I can help you with?"

Teddy felt guilty for bothering her, so he bought a pack of bubble gum. Then, just to make sure, he waited for another fifteen minutes behind the building for Albert to show.

Eventually, Teddy gave up and biked back toward Leslie Groves Park. As he worked his way down to the river, he kept his eyes peeled for Henry and his pals, in case they were still looking for him.

He found the sign for Leslie Groves Park, which looked older than he remembered, and he turned toward the river. But when he reached the edge of the park, he stopped, confused.

There was no Albert, no Henry, no anyone, and the park looked completely different. The dirt trail was now a paved walking path, and a vast lawn of fresh-smelling green grass had replaced the dusty scrub brush. A bright blue jungle gym stood where only tumbleweeds had been before, and a brick building with bathrooms had sprung up in the middle of it all. Even the island looked different. Before, it had been bare rocks, but now it was covered by saplings and wild grasses.

It was all wrong, and the impossibility of it made Teddy suddenly wonder if he'd dreamed the entire incident.

He rolled to a stop where he thought Albert had gone into the water. The flock of seagulls was still gathered on the island, the river was still dark and swift, and shadowy snags still lurked beneath its surface. But somehow these few familiar things were not comforting.

CHAPTER 3

Teddy biked back home, lost in thought about the bizarre change in the park and what might have happened to Albert. He stashed his bike in the backyard and hustled up to the deck, eager to get inside and make some sense of the afternoon. He was also ferociously thirsty after a couple hours in the desert sun.

The heat, he thought, *maybe it made me hallucinate.*

His mom had a pitcher of lemonade waiting for him. She'd been busy unpacking, and the room was littered with empty boxes.

"Hey." She greeted him with her artificial smile. "You

were gone for longer than I thought. Did you explore?"

"Yeah, a little," he replied.

"Where'd you go?"

"Down by the river."

"Oh," she said. "Be careful down there. The current is fast."

"I know."

She pulled a glass from the cupboard and poured it full of the unnaturally pink lemonade. Teddy took it with a quiet "thanks."

"Meet any other kids your age?"

"Yeah, one," he said, taking a huge gulp.

"So . . . what did you two do?"

"Threw rocks," Teddy said. He wanted to tell her more, but he didn't understand exactly what had happened, and he knew if he tried to explain, he'd probably wind up telling her that he'd nailed the neighborhood bully in the head.

"Was he, umm, cool?" she asked.

"Yeah. He seemed like a nice guy."

"That's great! Are you going to see him around?" she persisted.

"I don't know." It was an honest answer.

"Well, if he's nice, I sure hope so," she said. "It's important to pick good friends."

That night Teddy sat on his bed in shorts. It was an old sleigh-style bed, and the frame sat high off the ground, leaving a cavernous space underneath. A bulky gray comforter he'd had for years sat on top like a layer of protective armor. He hoped that after a decent night's sleep, he'd wake up with a reasonable explanation for the impossible events of the day.

His open window looked out at the old house next door and its massive sycamore tree. The tree's leaves were as big as dinner plates, with pointed tips that splayed out from the center.

Like hundreds of hands, Teddy thought, *reaching in all directions.*

A desert wind was rising, and swirling dust devils flung sand through the window into his second-floor room. One of the groping branches leaned in too, pushing the white curtain aside. But when Teddy rose to close the window, the branch retreated on a sudden gust.

The sun's glow lingered late on the summer horizon,

and it was almost ten o'clock when it faded completely. Teddy was exhausted, so he shut off his light with a loud *click*, climbed into bed, and pulled the comforter to his chin, settling in for his first night's sleep in his new home after a very uncomfortable first day.

Hours later, Teddy awoke to the rapping sound of tree branches clawing at the house. He blinked in the darkness and looked around, bleary-eyed. He almost reached out from under the covers for the bedside lamp, but then he noticed the open window. He could have sworn he'd closed it.

Could the wind have somehow blown it open? he wondered. But even half asleep in the middle of the night he knew that didn't make any sense.

He glanced at the clock—which read 2:30 A.M.—then back at the window. A small branch had twisted over the sill and disappeared down behind his bedside table. He peeked over the edge of the bed, and the rotten smell of wet, decaying leaves wafted over him.

It was then that he heard the scratching sound, like something with claws dragging itself across the new brown carpet. Teddy sucked in a breath—it was coming from under his bed.

The branch quivered behind the nightstand, making Teddy's heart pound as he imagined a rattlesnake curled around the end that was beneath his bed, shaking with its eagerness to strike. Or maybe a swarm of scorpions or black widow spiders pouring in on the branch from outside to scatter across his floor, creep up the walls, and crawl over his mattress.

Or could it be something even worse?

That was enough for Teddy. He dove off the bed wearing his comforter for protection and ran for the door. To his horror, the dust ruffle swished aside behind him, and something scratched over the carpet after him.

In the dark, he found the doorknob and desperately yanked at it, still shrouded in the comforter. The knob was new to Teddy, and he rattled it back and forth, horrified by the thought of some desert terror racing across the floor to leap on his back.

Just then, there was a sharp tug on his comforter. He didn't dare turn to look. To face the thing seemed more terrible than to simply curl up in the bedspread and pray that it went away.

But suddenly the knob turned, and he was in the hallway.

Teddy slammed the door behind him as hard as he could. Down the hall, his mom stumbled around the corner, eyes puffy, blindly groping toward the commotion.

"What the heck is going on?" she growled.

She snapped on the hall light to reveal Teddy wrapped up like a mummy in his comforter, holding the door closed.

"Teddy, why are you up?" she asked.

"Couldn't sleep?" he said lamely, squinting into the light.

His mother groaned. "My first day of work is tomorrow." She pushed open his door, eliciting a gasp from Teddy as he jumped behind her.

"What's wrong with you?" she asked.

"Something grabbed my comforter."

She pointed to where the gray bedspread was pinched in the jamb. "Something like the door?" She flipped on his light and walked into the room.

Before he could stop her, she knelt down on the floor and lifted the dust ruffle. "There's nothing here," she said.

As Teddy eased into the room, she held the ruffle up so that he could see. The floor beneath the bed was bare. He turned to the window. The branch that had climbed through it was gone.

"The window is still open," Teddy pointed out.

She closed it and turned the lock.

"Should we check the closet?" he suggested.

"Good night," she said, motioning him back to bed. She walked out, turning off the light and shutting the door behind her.

Teddy took a deep breath. He wanted to trust his mother's instinct that he was overreacting—after the events of the afternoon, he certainly didn't trust his own. Maybe it was just a bad combination of moving to a new town, having a weird day, and waking up in the middle of the night in an unfamiliar room, he thought. There was nothing there, just like she said.

But as he crept through the dark to his bed, the tree branch scraped across his window again. Now that his mom was gone, it almost seemed to want back in.

Teddy took two quick steps, leaped onto the mattress, and dove under the comforter. He pulled his arms and feet inside, a position from which he planned to ignore all further noises.

Still, it was going to be a long night.

CHAPTER 4

The next morning, Teddy robotically spooned cereal into his mouth, occasionally missing and spilling it on the table. He hadn't slept all night. Thankfully, nothing else weird had happened, and when the sun came up, the world seemed normal again.

Parks do not completely change in a half hour, Teddy thought, *and windows do not open themselves.*

He had almost convinced himself that the day before had been a quirky bad dream by the time his mom whirled into the kitchen at eight thirty and handed him an envelope.

"Two chores for you to do while I'm at work," she said. "Take this check over to the landlord at 613 Lynwood Court, and try to meet some more kids today. I saw a few outside, you know." She gave him a purposeful look. "Do not sit in the house and surf the internet all day. *Comprendez?*"

"*Si, señora,*" Teddy replied. He pocketed the letter and dumped half a spoonful of Sugar Flakes into his lap.

His mom gave him a kiss and set a cell phone on the table beside him. "Be good," she said. "My new work number is programmed into the phone." She grabbed her purse and headed for the door.

Teddy looked out the big front window. Some kids were riding skateboards over a homemade wood ramp down the block. But the air above the scorching blacktop was shimmering with heat, distorting their shapes into a grotesque mirage.

Teddy promptly headed upstairs to the study and settled into the desk chair beneath the air-conditioning duct to surf the internet.

He clicked through some video game sites, but they reminded him of Albert and made him feel strangely guilty.

So he typed in a search for Richland instead and found the local news website.

There was nothing about a missing chubby kid, which made him feel better. If Albert had run into real trouble, there would have been some mention of it. Teddy still felt queasy about hitting Henry Mulligan in the head with a rock—after just one day in town, he already had to watch his back. The changing park still bothered him too, but he decided to chalk it up to the heat and chaos of the encounter with Henry Mulligan at the river.

Teddy typed in a search for Leslie Groves Park, and Wikipedia articles about Richland and the Hanford Nuclear Site popped up. Teddy clicked on them and scrolled through the history sections, curious about his strange new home.

He discovered that Richland was originally no more than a few small desert farms irrigated by the Columbia River. That is, until 1943 when General Leslie R. Groves of the U.S. Army came to Washington hunting for a site to build nuclear reactors for the Second World War.

General Groves found the desert along the river to the

north of Richland ideal. He swooped in, seized a chunk of land half the size of Rhode Island, and forcibly removed two farm towns and a small Indian tribe from the area. The army turned Richland into a closed government town as part of the Manhattan Project—a secret nuclear program for which the Hanford nuclear plant produced radioactive plutonium for the "Fat Man" atomic bomb used to obliterate Nagasaki, Japan.

By 1945, twenty-five thousand workers were living near the nuclear plant, and everything about the town was related to atomic energy. The bowling alley was called Atomic Lanes, and the uniforms for the high school had mushroom clouds on them. The government itself built houses for the families and provided them with everything they needed, from free bus service to lightbulbs. The Feds even planted trees in the yards.

Teddy discovered that each type of government house was assigned a letter. A-houses were the biggest. There were B-houses, C-houses, and so on, all the way to Z. There were some pictures, and when he scrolled through them, he was surprised to find one that looked exactly like the old home next door. It was an A-house.

There was also a section in the article about radioactive waste. Weapons-grade plutonium and uranium were made in Richland during the Cold War years, and by the time the last reactor was shut down in 1987, 53 million gallons of radioactive waste had been left behind. In fact, waste was secretly dumped straight into the Columbia River until 1971, and contamination was found downstream as far west as the Oregon coast.

The worst incidence of radioactive waste dumping, known as the "Green Run," happened in 1949, when the government intentionally released a huge concentration of radiation into the air over two days, causing deadly diseases in humans and animals. In plants, the effect was unknown.

Teddy was almost through reading the article when a terrific bang startled him out of his chair. A distant clunk and hiss followed before the vent above him stopped pumping cold air.

He went downstairs to the kitchen. It already felt hot in the house, and it seemed to be getting hotter. He checked the thermometer in the window over the sink, which read almost eighty degrees inside. With any luck, he thought, the problem might be something obvious that he could fix—a handle he could reset, perhaps, like a breaker switch.

Outside the house, he found a green, sheet-metal air-conditioning unit against the beige wall. The unit was tilted at an odd angle, and blue fluid was bleeding down its exterior into a greasy puddle.

Teddy frowned—a leak was *not* something he could fix.

He got down on his hands and knees and looked under one end of the unit. The concrete pad to which the air conditioner was bolted was split down the middle. A tree root had cracked it and forced it apart, bending the thick metal housing of the unit in the process and tearing loose a copper hose.

There was clearly nothing he could do himself, so Teddy headed to the back door to go inside and call his mom. But when he tried the knob, it didn't turn. He shook it, but it was no use; the door had locked behind him.

With a sinking feeling, he realized that he'd left the Hide-a-Key inside. And the cell phone with his mom's new number was sitting beside it on the kitchen table.

Gazing through the window, Teddy cursed his own stupidity. He turned to his bike, which was leaning against the fence, and checked to make sure he still had the letter he was supposed to deliver. With no other options, he climbed on and pedaled off to find 613 Lynwood Court.

CHAPTER 5

Biking through the heat, Teddy rolled along Saint Street until he came to a sign that said LYNWOOD COURT. He skidded to a stop and pulled out the letter to confirm the address—613 Lynwood Court.

The street ended in a cul-de-sac with a circular expanse of blacktop ringed by a ribbon of gray sidewalk. But there were no homes around it. Instead, Teddy saw only wood frames jutting from bare concrete foundations, mere skeletons of houses not yet built. Open trenches almost ten feet deep had been dug through the sand and tumbleweeds between the home sites for a future sewer line.

Teddy checked the street name again. It was definitely correct. He coasted over the blacktop pavement into the unfinished cul-de-sac for a closer look.

"Hello?" he called. There didn't seem to be any workmen around, but considering the desert heat at midday, he didn't blame them.

Suddenly, he heard the frantic banging of what sounded like a hammer. Teddy homed in on the pounding. It was coming from the second home site on the left.

There was a boy in plaid shorts, long white socks, and a T-shirt with a cartoon Chevy van on it sitting on the half-finished second floor of the house. He was at the top of a staircase with no rail, holding a hammer, and he seemed to be taking great delight in whacking things around him at random.

"Excuse me," Teddy called out, waving to get the boy's attention, "do you know where 613 Lynwood Court is?"

The boy looked down at Teddy. "Who wants to know?" he asked.

"Me, I guess," Teddy replied. "I've got a letter for them."

"Next door." The boy smirked and pointed to the empty

foundation on the next lot over. "But I don't think they have a mailbox yet."

"Weird," Teddy mumbled, stuffing the letter back in his pocket. For a few moments he sat on his bike wondering what to do next, then the boy called down to him. "Hey, kid, you live in the neighborhood?"

"Since yesterday."

"Where?" he demanded.

"By the old abandoned A-house."

It seemed to be the right answer, because the boy nodded approvingly. "All right, then," he said. "Wanna see something groovy?"

Teddy hesitated. The boy seemed suspicious of him, and Teddy wasn't sure he should be messing around on a construction site. But then again he *did* want to see something groovy, so he parked his bike on the sidewalk and stepped onto the site.

"I'm Walter, and this whole block is my domain," the boy said as Teddy walked carefully up the incomplete stairs. "Until people move into the houses, I suppose. Isn't it great?"

"Will we get in trouble for being here?" Teddy asked, looking around. The floors were bare plywood with nails sticking up all over the place, and there was scrap wood scattered about. There were no walls either—only vertical two-by-fours every two feet that formed the frame of the house—and the roof wasn't on yet. It looked like a big, square wooden jail cell.

Walter ignored Teddy's question. "The workers leave stuff lying around when they go home."

"Really? Like what?"

"Just today I found two lighters and a *Hot Rod* magazine—you should see the new Camaro." Walter held up the magazine, dropping the centerfold open so Teddy could see the car. It looked like an old Camaro to him.

"But that's not all," Walter said, wiggling his eyebrows. "The construction guys also leave their tools."

"What's so cool about that?" Teddy asked.

With a grin, Walter raised the hammer and hurled it past Teddy's head into a sheet of wallboard. It smashed a hole through the sheet, and a cloud of white dust exploded into the air.

"Ha! You flinched!" Walter bent over, laughing hysterically as the wallboard dust settled on Teddy like fallout from a bomb.

"Fun stuff, huh?" Walter said, wiping tears from his eyes. "Now you do it. Go ahead. I won't flinch. I *don't* flinch."

The damage made Teddy feel uneasy, but he had to admit, the hammer-throwing explosion was sort of cool. A screwdriver lay on the stairs. Teddy debated picking it up. He was pretty sure he could throw as well as Walter.

"C'mon, chicken," Walter chided.

I'm not a chicken, Teddy thought.

He snatched up the screwdriver and hurled it end over end between Walter's legs. The sharp tip buried itself in the stairs just below Walter's plaid shorts. It stuck there, vibrating back and forth.

He didn't mean to throw it so close, but Walter loved it. "Whoa! Faaaaa-ar out," he cackled.

"Uh-oh," Teddy said. "I think I damaged the stairway." There was a large crack in the board where the tip of the screwdriver had stuck in.

"Yeah." Walter grinned. "Now we're talkin'!" He pulled

out one of the lighters he'd found and set the end of a short wooden dowel ablaze. "Look, it's the Olympic torch."

Teddy watched it burn, mesmerized for a moment by the dancing flame. But as he watched the torch burn, he was horrified to notice that the hand Walter held it with was missing its index finger.

"You like fire?" Walter said knowingly.

Teddy shook his head. The sun-dried wood around them looked dangerously flammable, and Walter's missing finger was downright creepy. "I think we should put it out," he said.

Walter grinned again. "Oh, yeah? I'll bet I can set fires faster than you can put them out."

With that, he romped off through the half-built house, thrusting the torch out at random and singeing the two-by-four framing and plywood floors as he went. In his wake, he left charred black marks, a burnt smell, and bursts of laughter.

Feeling a strange mix of exhilaration and guilt, Teddy followed, trying to keep up. Mostly the flames didn't catch, but once Teddy had to stop and stomp out a newspaper that was starting to send up tendrils of smoke.

When he had made a full circuit through the house, Walter darted between the two-by-four framing and leaped from the second floor down into a huge pile of dirt on the ground. He ran to the next unfinished house to resume his scorching.

Teddy hustled down the stairs behind him, his excitement fading as Walter showed no signs of stopping. He ran to the next house, desperately following the trail of smoldering wood and black scars his new friend had left behind.

"Walter! You've gotta stop!" he yelled.

When he entered the next unfinished home, Teddy found the discarded torch on the floor. But Walter himself had disappeared out the other side and was nowhere to be seen.

Then he heard Walter's voice. "Down here, slowpoke!"

Teddy walked to the edge of the sewer trench between the building sites and spotted Walter standing at the bottom, ten feet down.

"Fun stuff, huh?" Walter said again.

"No," Teddy said. "I don't think setting fires is fun. We should get out of here before the workmen come back."

"Looky here." Walter picked up a shovel and smacked the dirt-and-rock wall of the trench. A small section of wall caved in, and he leaped aside as it scattered rocks across his feet.

"Dare ya," Walter said.

"Dare me what?"

"Dare ya to make a bigger avalanche."

"I don't think so," Teddy said.

"What, no guts?" Walter snorted. He raised the shovel again. "Scaredy cat?"

"I wouldn't keep doing that," Teddy warned.

"No. *You* wouldn't."

With a smirk, Walter swung the shovel at the wall right below Teddy's feet. A refrigerator-sized chunk of earth broke away, and Teddy leaped back as the bank caved in beneath his shoes.

Below, Walter dodged the tumbling debris, diving along the bottom of the trench as rocks and dirt fell behind him. Once it stopped, he stood up, laughing hysterically.

"That was awesome!" he cried. "C'mon down and try it."

From the edge of the trench, Teddy surveyed the wide, crescent-shaped scar Walter had made in the dirt. Exposed rocks and the crooked ends of still-quivering tree roots jutted out.

"No way," Teddy said, looking over his shoulder for his bicycle. It suddenly seemed like a good time to say good-bye to Walter.

"Please," Walter said in a suddenly serious tone. "This is my last chance."

Teddy wasn't sure exactly what Walter meant, but shook his head—there was no way he was going down there. At that moment, the wall of the trench suddenly shifted. The tree roots sticking out of the wall jerked and twitched, knocking small stones loose, and a long crack began to snake through the dirt near Teddy's feet at the edge of the pit.

"Run!" Teddy yelled as Walter watched the crack widen above him.

Walter didn't run. He stood in place with a resigned look on his face and reached up, pleading. "Help me, Teddy. Grab my hand."

But Teddy wasn't listening anymore. Instead, he stared in horror as the gnarled, handlike tree roots writhed forth from the wall of the trench and grabbed Walter's ankles and arms, holding him in place. Then the wall collapsed, covering his new friend with ten feet of dirt and rock.

CHAPTER 6

A wailing patrol car banked hard onto Saint Street. Teddy waved from the sidewalk in front of the house at 550 Saint—a half block from the construction site—where he'd run to call the police.

The car screeched to a stop. "Where's the buried kid?" a police officer shouted out the window.

"Down there in Lynwood Court!" Teddy yelled back. The car lurched forward and disappeared around the corner. Teddy hopped on his bike and followed it down the street.

When he arrived at the cul-de-sac, the officer was pacing beside his car in front of a series of completely finished homes with lawns, welcome mats, and cars in their driveways. The Lynwood Court sign was in the same place, but it was faded, not shiny and new. And there were no construction sites.

Teddy wheeled his bike up a driveway and kicked a garage door that hadn't been there before in disbelief. It was real.

"Calm down there, son," the officer said. His blue uniform read BARNES across the pocket.

"But it was here," Teddy said.

"What was here?" Officer Barnes asked.

"Lynwood Court."

"This *is* Lynwood Court."

An ambulance squealed to a stop behind the patrol car, and Teddy began to feel the need to explain something he didn't understand.

"Yeah, I know," he said. "But the houses were under construction before."

"Before what?"

"Before I called."

"Young man," Officer Barnes said, "Lynwood Court was under construction forty years ago."

A fire truck pulled up now too, its crew leaping out to assist with the horrible emergency Teddy had reported. As Teddy watched them, shifting from foot to foot and wishing he were somewhere else, he began to feel sick to his stomach. The homes in the cul-de-sac before him *did* look forty years old.

Paramedics and firemen joined Teddy and Officer Barnes on the sidewalk, huffing from their mad dash to the scene with their heavy equipment.

"Where's the trench?" one of the firemen asked.

Teddy shrugged. "It was between the houses around here somewhere, but now it's all lawn."

Officer Barnes harrumphed. "Okay, so you saw a boy buried in a trench that you can't find now. What was his name?"

"Walter."

"Walter what?"

Teddy sighed. "I don't know."

"I see. So a boy you don't know disappeared in a hole

you can't find." Barnes shook his head and waved the emergency crews away. He opened a notebook and took out a pen. "And what's your name, son?" he grumbled.

Teddy's shoulders slumped. He dropped his head onto his chest; he couldn't look Barnes in the eye anymore. "Teddy," he said.

CHAPTER 7

Once the emergency crews had cleared out, Officer Barnes drove Teddy home. He was reluctant to leave Teddy stranded outside his house without a parent, and it took Teddy a long time to explain that he didn't know the location of his mother's new high-security job and that her phone number was locked inside the house. He also declined Barnes's offer to break in for him, and, finally, Barnes had simply left with his name and home phone number so that he could call Teddy's mom later, probably to tell her how much trouble Teddy had gotten himself into by telling such a ferocious lie.

Teddy was still outside on the porch when his mother pulled up after work to find him sitting there sunburned as red as a lobster. He didn't tell her about Walter—he wasn't exactly sure what *to* tell her. Instead, he simply said that the air conditioner had broken, he'd taken the check over to Lynwood Court, then he'd hung out in front of the house, all of which were true.

If I'm lucky, he thought, *Officer Barnes will get busy and forget about me.*

His mom made spaghetti for dinner, and Teddy silently plowed through two full plates to make up for missing lunch. As he ate, he listened to her talk about her new job at the nuclear plant.

"I like the lab here," she was saying, "and I'll get a raise after my probationary period. Until then, we'll have to watch our budget. Thank goodness you're responsible enough that I can leave you home without—"

"Can nuclear waste make people hallucinate?" Teddy interrupted.

"Well, no," she answered, seeming surprised about his concern with toxic waste, "although it *can* be dangerous."

"How?"

She thought for a moment. "Some highly radioactive material gives off energy in large, lethal doses—it kills things. Low-level material takes a longer time to decay, but the energy still seeps out, and it can mutate living cells. They're very careful with it nowadays, though."

"How long does it take to decay?"

"Why do you ask?"

"Just interested in your new job," Teddy fibbed.

"It varies," she answered. "It has what they call a half-life. Half the energy of something radioactive is drained over a period of time. It takes that same amount of time again to drain half of what's left, and so on. The energy dwindles until there's almost nothing left." She paused to take a mouthful of spaghetti. "But don't worry," she reassured him. "I work in a very safe area at the plant."

Teddy nodded that he understood. But it wasn't an area at the plant he was worried about.

CHAPTER 8

The next morning, Teddy sat at the kitchen table as his mom got ready for work. He'd lain awake puzzling over the disappearances of Walter and Albert, all the while listening to the branches clawing at his bedroom window. Either the boys in the neighborhood were playing very disturbing tricks on him or his mind was, but he couldn't figure out which, and for the second night in a row, he hadn't slept a wink.

His mom noticed. "So I take it you haven't had the best first couple of days here," she said.

"Not the best, no," Teddy admitted.

She rose from the table. "I'm too new to ask for time off work or I'd stay here with you, but listen, I want you to stick close to home today, okay?"

"No problem," Teddy mumbled, and he meant it. He wasn't going near rivers, construction sites, or anyplace remotely dangerous.

"Okay," his mom said, giving him a good-bye kiss for which he felt too old. "A repairman is coming later to look at the air conditioner."

An hour later, the repairman was bent under the air-conditioning unit with his skinny rump in the air. Teddy stood nearby holding a length of new pipe.

The repairman tossed out a piece of old metal pipe from the unit that was tattered and mushroomed out at one end as though it had exploded.

"Here's your problem," he said. "Tree roots in your pipes."

"What?"

The man stood up, one greasy hand on his pockmarked chin. The name tag on his coveralls said HANK.

"You deaf?" he said.

"No. It just seems weird."

"It's common, really." Hank yawned, flipping his stringy hair out of his eyes. "Over time, they get into everything."

"Why?"

"Looking for water, usually. In the desert those roots will get into sewers, plumbing, even crawl all the way to the river. Can't believe this one went after the air conditioner, though. Must be desperate."

Hank rummaged in his pocket, pulled out a pocket knife, and began to clean his fingernails. He turned his narrow green eyes on Teddy. "You know, you look familiar, kid," he said as he rubbed an old scar on his forehead. "Do I know you?"

"I don't think so," Teddy said. "I just moved here."

Hank shrugged and snatched the new pipe from Teddy. He plopped back down to install it, hoisting his rump back up in the air.

Teddy stared at the old mutilated pipe. "This is completely destroyed."

"Yeah," Hank agreed from under the air-conditioning unit. "They pry their way in. Powerful things, though they usually just crack stuff. That little number looks like a nuclear bomb went off in it."

Hank finished attaching the new pipe and scooted out from under the air conditioner, wiping his hands on his shirt.

Teddy nodded, troubled by how easily simple tree roots had forced him out of his home.

"Will they come back?" he asked.

Hank shrugged. "Maybe, eventually. No one can give guarantees, kid."

CHAPTER 9

Once Hank left, Teddy retreated inside the house. But he knew deep down he couldn't simply cower in his home. If the tree was trying to get in through the window and sabotaging the air conditioner to force him outside, he had to figure out why.

Summoning his courage—it was just a tree, after all— Teddy pushed the kitchen door open and peeked outside. He crept to the edge of his backyard, where the massive sycamore rose above him on the other side of the fence, its cracked wood riddled with scars from the many decades of nature's abuse. It seemed to frown down at him, healthy but somehow unsatisfied.

"What do you want?" Teddy asked.

The sycamore, of course, did not reply. It only swayed in the hot desert breeze, and Teddy instantly felt stupid for talking to it. He turned to go back inside.

Just then, something hit Teddy in the head.

"Oww," he grumbled as a sycamore seed ball bounced to the ground beside him. It was the size of a golf ball, and its surface bristled with pointy seeds. Teddy looked up to see where the ball had dropped from and saw a boy sitting on a branch above him almost completely hidden by leaves.

"Hey, what's cookin'?" the boy said. His grin was not quite a smirk, so Teddy couldn't decide if he'd meant to throw the sycamore ball hard enough to hurt him or just to get Teddy's attention.

The kid was about Teddy's age, but looked a little taller, and he wore long wool knickers and an argyle patterned sweater-vest over a white shirt. His outfit made him look like an old-time schoolboy dressed for fall instead of summer.

"Why'd you do that?" Teddy said, rubbing his head where he'd been struck by the sycamore ball.

"I didn't," the boy replied. "The tree dropped it."

"It's a pretty odd coincidence," Teddy said, "seeing as you were sitting *directly* above me when it fell straight down and hit me *directly* in the middle of the head."

"A wiseacre, eh?" the boy said. "I like that."

Before Teddy could reply, he heard a long, low groan, like the creaking timbers of a massive wooden ship. He whirled around to find the source, but it seemed to come from all around him, even up from the ground.

"Are you making that sound?" he asked.

The kid chuckled. "Do I look like I could make a sound that grand?"

As Teddy stood trying to figure out what might make such a *grand* sound, he spotted a large branch above his head swaying in the breeze. Only it wasn't just moving back and forth—it was also moving down toward him, creaking and groaning as it came. The branch descended to within arm's reach of Teddy and stopped directly in front of him.

Teddy leaped back. "Did you see that?" he gasped. "That branch just moved!"

The kid nodded and slid from his own branch onto the base of the moving branch, perching himself so that his legs dangled over the side. "Sure. The wind blows. They make noise. They go up. They come down. They move side to side. It's no big deal."

Teddy eyed the tree suspiciously, unconvinced that it was just the wind.

"Swell, huh?" the boy said. "It's the biggest tree on the block." He waved a foot toward the smaller birch, willow, and fruit trees lining the long street.

"You live near here?"

"Yeah," Teddy said. "I just moved in next door."

"I'm Eugene," the boy announced, "but everyone just calls me Sloot. I'm pretty much in charge around here, because I've been here the longest."

Teddy had a sudden brainstorm. "Hey, since you've lived here so long, do you know Walter or Albert?"

"Of course," Sloot said.

"Really?" Teddy asked, excited and a little surprised that someone finally knew what he was talking about. "I just met them, but they both kind of disappeared."

"Nonsense," Sloot said. "I saw them this morning."

CHAPTER 10

Teddy let out a deep breath as relief washed over him. Somehow Walter hadn't been buried and Albert had gotten away.

"That's so great . . . !" he exclaimed, the words pouring out of him now. "Whoa. You wouldn't believe what I thought happened to them. I mean, Walter must have totally fooled me, because it seemed so real when he—"

"They're fine!" Sloot interrupted angrily. "Walter's as weird as ever, and Albert's still a lard-butt. Do we really need to blather on about them?"

"Uh, no, I guess not," Teddy mumbled, taken aback by Sloot's change in tone.

"So, do you like this place?" Sloot asked quickly, changing the subject.

"No offense, but I think it's a little weird."

Sloot laughed. "Boy howdy, you got that right. The G-men built this town from nuthin' right up out of the desert a few years ago."

"G-men?"

"Government men. Do your folks work at the nuke-u-lar project? You can tell me. I'll keep it under my hat."

"My mom does, yeah," Teddy said. "But I don't think it's a secret."

Sloot shrugged. "Well, loose lips sink ships, as they say. My dad works there too, but if he knew I said something about it he'd give me a knuckle sandwich, so don't *you* go tellin' anybody." Sloot made a fist and gave Teddy a sudden fierce look.

"Ooo-kay," Teddy said carefully.

Sloot nodded, satisfied. "You coming up?" he said, instantly turning cheery again.

Teddy eyed the huge tree. It looked like a long way up,

and Sloot's sudden changes in mood made him nervous. "Wasn't planning to."

"Aww, c'mon," Sloot cooed. "If you take a gander from the top, you can see all the way to the river. Branches are thin up there, but they might hold you. You're nice and skinny."

"Sounds like a good way to get killed."

Sloot went quiet for a moment. "Pretty good, yeah," he finally said. "A fella could climb up there, and nobody would find him . . . ever." Then he looked over his shoulder toward the trunk of the tree and the A-house beyond. "Well, my time's about done. You coming up or not?"

"Uh, I think *not.*"

Sloot frowned, his face turning dark again with a flash of anger. "I'm not sure I heard you right. Did you tell me no?"

"Uh, well, yes," Teddy spluttered. "I mean, yes, I said no."

Sloot rolled his eyes. "Well, I can't sit around flappin' my lips all day with some meatball like you who can't make up his mind."

"But I *did* make up my mind."

Sloot stood up on the branch. He gave Teddy a long look. "No, you haven't." He stepped out to the middle of the branch, which swayed upward in the breeze, lifting him into the tree as if it were a small elevator.

Teddy stared up at the tree. His instinct, common sense, and rattled nerves all told him to walk away and forget about Sloot. But instead, the longer he gazed into the syca-more, the more he felt it drawing him closer—the same way the A-house had pulled him to it the day he'd arrived.

He marveled at how it could be so unnaturally green, its leaves so strangely vibrant and healthy compared to the dead yard. The tree was so full of life that it felt inviting. More and more, Teddy found that he *did* want to climb up into it. He wanted to see Richland from the top.

Maybe just halfway to start with, he thought. *What would be the harm?*

Like a moth attracted to a bright light, Teddy found himself walking toward the trunk of the tree. The large branch creaked in the breeze, lowering itself again.

They go up, they come down . . . no big deal, Sloot had as-sured him.

Teddy climbed onto the branch, and it immediately

lifted him into the tree. In an instant, he was ten feet off the ground, climbing through the limbs.

As he moved higher, the soft leaves brushed his arms and caressed his face. Branches seemed to bend toward him so he could reach them easily and keep climbing up. The air felt cooler as he rose in the protective shade of the tree, and because he couldn't see more than five feet in any direction, the outside world soon seemed miles away.

"Sloot?" he called.

"Up here," Sloot's faint voice replied.

He still couldn't see Sloot, so he kept working his way higher. Somehow, the climb didn't seem dangerous. The branches felt solid beneath his feet. In fact, it was so easy that it felt almost as though the branches were passing him up from one to the next.

"Up where?" He called.

"Keep coming." Sloot's words sounded muffled, like he had leaves in his mouth.

"Show me where you are," Teddy said, wondering if Sloot was kidding around, perhaps lurking somewhere nearby to jump out at him or smack him with another syca-more ball.

As Teddy spoke, the branches above him parted, revealing a huge, gaping knothole in the trunk of the tree. The hole was more than three feet across and rimmed with a thick, swollen band of purplish bark that glistened like the wet lips of a fish. There sat Sloot with his rump in the hole and his upper body and legs hanging out so that he looked folded in the middle.

"You're almost here," he said eagerly.

"This is getting a little high for me," Teddy replied from below. "I just wanted to see the view."

"Sure. Relax. You're high enough now for a look around." Sloot pointed out through the thick branches, and the hot breeze eased them apart.

Suddenly, Teddy could see for miles. He immediately spotted the scrubby park by the river to the east where he'd met Albert. But when he looked north, Walter's construction site was missing. In fact, while he didn't know the neighborhood well yet, there were a lot fewer rooftops than he expected. And there were no homes at all where he thought Lynwood Court should be—only open desert.

"It looks a lot smaller," Teddy said.

"It used to be," Sloot said from above him. "Okay, you've

seen enough, and I'm about out of time here. Come on up. I want to show you something."

The branches on the tree shifted again, obscuring Teddy's view of the town. Inside the thick limbs, it once again grew shady, almost dark. The leaves were still touching Teddy as they had on the way up, but now they felt probing instead of caressing. He felt one inch behind his ear and another slither up his sleeve into his armpit, where their strangely wet surfaces stuck to his skin, and they clung like leeches.

Teddy turned to Sloot for help, but Sloot was gone. The knothole in which he'd been sitting yawned open, bigger and dripping wet now, and Teddy was glad he wasn't any closer to it.

Just then, the limbs supporting Teddy's weight rose, lifting him up toward the black opening like hands shoveling food to a drooling mouth.

Teddy glanced around, frantic, and shouted. "Help! Sloot, help me!" But he was no longer there, and Teddy was too high for anyone else to reach him in time.

He had no choice. Teddy ripped away the leaves clinging to his flesh, tore himself loose from the limbs that held him, and jumped.

He didn't fall far—there were too many branches. The next one down caught him on his stomach while he clawed for a handhold on another. But when he got hold of the branch, it jerked him upward again.

Teddy let go instantly, dropping through the tree again. He felt a branch slam into his shin. Another whacked his head. As he bounced back and forth between limbs like a pinball, he thought he might be pummeled to death before he reached the ground.

At last, Teddy tumbled clear of the huge lower branches. He saw the ground coming at him out of the corner of his eye and managed to squirm around so that he could try to land on all fours.

The impact stunned him, and he instantly hurt in places he didn't even know existed. But there was no time to see if he'd broken anything—he was lying right beneath the tree, and two huge branches were swaying back down toward him. Frantically, Teddy dragged himself to his feet and stumbled across the yard toward his house.

CHAPTER 11

Bruised and shaking, Teddy took a shortcut through the garage. As he hurried past the shelves, he grabbed a hatchet and a small plastic pump-spray bottle of weed killer, which he stuffed in his pocket.

For the next three hours, Teddy cowered in his room. He kept an eye on the tree from his bedroom window, hatchet in hand. But it didn't move again, and there was no sign of Eugene Sloot.

After a while, Teddy calmed down enough to consider what had happened in the tree, as well as all the other strange events of the last two days. Sloot was the third kid to mysteriously disappear. But, like the others, Teddy didn't think he could prove it to anyone—he couldn't even prove it to himself. Each crime scene changed as soon as he left. Even the sycamore just looked like a motionless tree now— nobody would believe it had tried to eat him.

Keeping an eye on the tree, he quickly moved into the study, sat down at the computer, and scanned the local news again. There was still nothing about recently missing kids.

Back in his own room, he checked his window latch again. There was no question now that he was unsafe even in his own house. Whatever ghastly fate was stalking the other boys, it had come as close as next door to get Sloot.

I have to do something, Teddy decided. But it was all a horrible puzzle, and he still had no idea where to look for answers or what to do next.

That is, until the mail slot clanked in the foyer.

Teddy crept downstairs to see what had arrived, and lying on the floor in the entryway beneath the slot, he found a bill for the air conditioner from Mulligan Repair Service.

"Mulligan?" he said to himself, trying it aloud as he walked the bill toward his mom's desk. It sounded familiar.

He recalled that the repairman's name tag on his uniform read "Hank."

"Hank Mulligan," Teddy said, wrapping his mouth around the entire name. But as he ran his finger down to the bottom of the page, he realized that Hank was a nickname. He found the man's full proper name printed below the signature line.

Henry Mulligan.

CHAPTER 12

Teddy biked madly down Saint Street, out toward the desert, then hung a left. If his own repairman was Henry Mulligan, the kid he'd hit with the rock had to be Henry Mulligan, Jr.

After all, Teddy thought, *how many Henry Mulligans can there be in Richland?*

Mr. Mulligan would have answers about his son. He probably knew all about Leslie Groves Park, too, and maybe even the other boys.

The mobile home park Teddy had seen when they first came into town was less than a mile from the corner where he turned. He covered the distance in record time and skidded to a stop in front of the park.

He recognized the faded sign over the cracked blacktop pavement leading into the park from two days earlier. The old trailers looked like they had just been plopped on top of the desert sand and sagebrush and simply left to rot.

He bit his lip and pedaled in, winding his way through a grid of streets between the mobile homes until he came to the return address on the repair bill. Before he could chicken out, he walked straight up onto the porch and knocked.

Nobody answered.

Teddy shuffled around on the porch, rising on his tiptoes to look in the window. He couldn't see anything through the dingy curtain, but he couldn't leave, either— no questions had been answered.

Taking a deep breath, Teddy pushed the door. It squeaked open, and he grimaced as a dry heat wafted out. It seemed hotter in the trailer than it was outside in the sun.

"Hello?" he called just to be sure nobody was home. When he again received no answer, he took another deep breath and slipped inside.

It was stuffy in the trailer, and all of the blinds were closed. The only furniture in the front room was a ratty old couch—the sort that looked like it would have stale corn chips buried in the cushions. It sat across from an old big-screen TV that took up an entire wall.

Teddy gave the room a long look. He still wasn't sure what he was searching for, but felt he'd know it when he saw it. Whatever it was, it wasn't in the front room.

"Hello? Mr. Mulligan?" Teddy called again. The place was small—he could see all the way to the other end. It would only take a few more steps to get a quick peek in the other rooms, so he started down the short hallway to the back of the trailer.

The bedroom on the left had a pair of long, narrow work boots sitting on the floor—clearly not a kid's shoes—so Teddy continued down the hall. He walked nervously past two doors, one of which opened into a bathroom. The other was a utility closet.

When he reached the final room at the rear, he looked around, puzzled. It seemed to be an office, and there was no kid's bedroom.

Actually, the office was no more than a room with a

dresser that had a stack of papers piled on top and a cheap folding chair in front of it. But it occurred to Teddy that there still might be clues here.

Every dad has photo albums, he thought. *And in such a small trailer, any albums with pictures of Mulligan's son would have to be in this room.*

Teddy started with the top drawer. There he found an old, rusty folding knife and a tattered junior-high yearbook from 1980 sitting in a cardboard box. He picked up the knife and turned it over, examining the blade. Albert had said Henry carried a knife, but the one Teddy held looked far too old.

Next, he took the yearbook out and flipped through each grade to find Mr. Mulligan's teenage photo from three decades ago. It turned up in the eighth-grade section. Teddy expected that Mr. Mulligan's picture would look a bit like the boy he'd hit with the rock at the river.

But Teddy was wrong—the photo looked exactly like him.

Henry Mulligan's sneering face was surrounded by long, stringy hair and marred by exactly the same acne. He was even wearing the same muscle shirt. A chill ran up Teddy's spine as he remembered how the forty-year-old repairman had a pockmarked complexion and an old scar above his green eyes.

As Teddy's heart raced, the yearbook shook in his nervous hands. He'd come looking for answers and he'd found one, but not one anyone could believe, even him. The boy he'd hit with a rock and his repairman were the same person!

He picked up Mulligan's rusty knife again, and with an ache in the pit of his stomach, he realized that it was the same knife the young bully had used to terrorize kids thirty years ago.

Then Teddy had an even more disturbing thought.

He turned back to the seventh-graders in the thirty-year-old yearbook. By now he had a creeping feeling that he should get out of the trailer soon, but he had to check one last thing.

On page ten in the seventh-grade section, he found what he was looking for. A chubby boy in the first row of the old photos grinned up at him with a familiar squinchy-eyed smile.

It was Albert Barker.

CHAPTER 13

At first, Teddy refused to believe it. But there was a memorial page for Albert, the kind schools include in the back of the yearbook when a student dies during the year. It named his favorite movie as *Star Wars*, and it had pictures of him goofing around at the school in his old bell-bottom jeans. There was also a short, photocopied newspaper article listing him as missing.

On the facing page there was a photo of a ceremony at the cemetery Teddy and his mom had passed coming into town. It showed a row of stone markers, one of them with Albert's name on it and flowers on the ground below.

As Teddy stared at the picture, still in disbelief, he heard the unmistakable crunching sound of tires on gravel outside. He ran for the door, but it was too late.

An old Ford pickup rolled to a stop directly in front of the porch. Through the window in the front door, Teddy saw Henry Mulligan step out of the truck. It was the same Henry he'd hit two days earlier with a rock, only grown up—the same man who'd found tree roots in his air conditioner's pipes.

Henry stomped toward the front porch, but stopped when he saw the bicycle in his yard. He frowned and took a shiny new folding knife out of his pocket. With a quick flick of his wrist, he flipped open the blade. "Someone there?" he called as he stepped up onto the porch. "Somebody's gonna get stuck if they ain't careful," he added.

His heart pounding, Teddy ducked into the coat closet, hoping that Henry would pass by so he could make a run for it. As he heard Henry enter the trailer, he realized he was still holding Henry's rusty old knife. He couldn't drop it, for fear it would make a sound, so he stuffed it in his pocket. But as he did, it hit the hard plastic nozzle of the little weed killer bottle and made a clicking sound.

"Aha!" Henry said, and he grabbed the handle of the closet door.

Teddy didn't have a plan, but he was dead certain he was about to be stabbed. So when the door flew open he did the only thing he could think to do—he sprayed weed killer in Henry Mulligan's face.

CHAPTER 14

It didn't take long to reach the cemetery. It was only a mile up the road from Desert Oasis, and Teddy's adrenalin was pumping.

I've taken on the town bully twice, he thought as he pedaled. *And I survived both times.*

But he didn't feel proud—just terrified and a bit guilty. Fortunately, Henry Mulligan hadn't gotten a good look at him. Teddy was sure of that. Henry had gone straight to the floor with his hands over his eyes, yelling, "Whoever you are, you're dead!"

As Teddy rode through the cemetery gates, he looked

for the row of lonely headstones he saw in the ceremony photo in the yearbook. He was pretty sure he could recognize it, because he'd noticed there were no spaces in front of the stones for graves—they were missing persons memorials only.

He found the distinctively narrow row near the back of the lot. Names were carved in the face of the granite monuments along with the dates each person was born and disappeared.

Teddy walked his bike along the row, looking for Albert's stone. Most of the missing were adults, so the dates on one stone caught Teddy's eye:

LAWRENCE COX 1948–1960

Lawrence Cox had been twelve years old when he'd gone missing. Just like Teddy.

As he continued along the row, Teddy paid more attention to the dates. He was surprised to find two *more* twelve-year-olds.

OLIVER STRAND 1988–2000

JOEY LANDI 1978–1990

Not only were all three of the kids twelve, they were all boys like him. Teddy glanced over his shoulder nervously, suddenly wondering if it was a good idea to be wandering alone in the graveyard. He looked around for threatening trees, but all he saw were rows of small, well-trimmed saplings.

Teddy quickly moved on, and, a few steps later, he found what he was looking for:

ALBERT BARKER 1968–1980

As he feared, Albert was also twelve years old when he disappeared thirty years ago—exactly the age he'd appeared to be when Teddy met him by the river just two days earlier.

For a full minute, Teddy stood motionless in front of the stone, his logic struggling with the clues in front of him, arguing against the impossible conclusions they led to. Then he glanced to his left at the next stone over:

WALTER FICK 1958–1970

Teddy knelt down beside it and ran his hand across the carved surface. He hadn't known the last name of the crazy boy named Walter he'd met at the construction site, but now he had the queasy feeling that it must have been Fick. And according to the stone, twelve-year-old Walter Fick had disappeared forty years ago, the year Lynwood Court was built and exactly ten years before Albert.

There were a few more stones Teddy hadn't seen yet. He almost didn't want to look, but he needed to see if there was one more name that he knew.

He found it at the end of the row, an old, weather-beaten rock with the name chipped out. Its ragged inscription read:

EUGENE SLOOT 1938–1950

In the quiet of the cemetery, Teddy whispered the one conclusion even his logic couldn't deny: "I've been hanging out with dead boys."

CHAPTER 15

As Teddy biked home, he tried to sort through the nightmarish clues he'd uncovered. The boys' memorial stones were scattered at random among other names and different ages, but the pattern was clear: Each boy had been twelve years old when he went missing, and the boys had vanished at ten-year intervals.

This last realization made Teddy skid to a stop in the middle of the street as he was struck by a horrific theory. He himself had been born in 1998, and it was now 2010—he was twelve, and it had been exactly ten years since the last disappearance.

I'm next, he thought.

When Teddy arrived home, dripping sweat from the heat and the terror of his discovery, his mom met him at the back door. He almost started to tell her everything he'd found out, but she spoke first.

"Teddy, there's a police officer here."

Teddy froze. "What for?" he replied as though it shouldn't mean anything to him.

"He said you might know," his mother continued, sounding suspicious. "Come with me."

Teddy followed his mom through the house to the foyer, where he peeked out from behind her. There on the porch stood Officer Barnes.

"Hello, Teddy. How are you?" Barnes smiled. Even though it was one hundred degrees outside, he was wearing his dark blue shirt and long blue pants.

"Hot," Teddy replied.

"And it might get hotter too," Barnes said, pulling out his notebook. "Mind if I ask you a few questions?"

"About what?"

"I mentioned to your mom that we met over at Lynwood Court yesterday. Told her it was no big deal and how, being new in town, you had just gotten lost."

"Thanks," Teddy answered, unsure of what else to say.

"But now I'd like to talk about the Desert Oasis trailer park. You know the place?"

"It's on the way into town, right?" Teddy's mom chimed in.

Barnes grimaced. "I actually wanted to know if *Teddy* knew. You been up there lately, Teddy?"

Teddy didn't want to lie. "I was at the cemetery near there, if that's what you mean."

His mom cocked her head in surprise.

"A man in the park described a blue bicycle near his trailer, a bike a lot like the one I've seen you riding. His name is Mulligan. You know him?"

"That sounds familiar," Teddy's mom interrupted. "Wasn't that the name of the air-conditioner repairman?"

Barnes groaned. "I really want to hear this from Teddy, Ms. Matthews," he said. "Is that your repairman, Teddy?"

"Yeah, I think that was his name."

"Okay," Barnes said, scribbling in his book. "Any reason for you to be at his trailer? Maybe you wanted to talk to him? Possibly checked inside to see if he was home?"

Teddy didn't take the bait. "No. No good reason."

Barnes turned to his mom. "Is Teddy unsupervised all day, Ms. Matthews?" he asked.

"He's a good boy," she replied quickly. Teddy could tell she didn't like the question.

"All right," Barnes said amiably. "Just looking for witnesses. Mr. Mulligan was assaulted by someone he found in his trailer. He didn't get a good look at the guy, but thought he was young. He said that the suspect had rummaged his office and that he was missing a knife he'd had since he was a teenager."

Teddy stiffened, realizing that Mulligan's old knife was still in his pocket.

"Teddy doesn't carry knives," his mom said.

"Assault during the course of a burglary is very serious," Barnes continued, "so we're investigating. But Mr. Mulligan is not the most reliable person I know, either." Barnes snapped his notebook closed. "He could have gotten it wrong."

"Is that all?" Teddy's mom asked.

"Can I talk to Teddy privately for a moment?" Barnes requested.

She looked at Teddy, and he nodded that it was okay. "I'll be in the kitchen," she said, and she went into the house.

Barnes walked Teddy down to his patrol car. "I checked on that name you mentioned—Walter. A boy named Walter Fick went missing in 1970, which matches up with the date that Lynwood Court was a construction zone."

"How do you know that?"

"Investigation. I'm a policeman, remember? But Walter was supposed to have disappeared near Davidson Avenue."

"No, it was at the building site," Teddy said before he could stop himself.

"Well, that's unlikely," Barnes said. "But interesting."

"What do you know about Albert Barker or Eugene Sloot?" Teddy blurted out.

Barnes quickly noted the names in his book. "Nothing yet," he said, "but I will." He opened the patrol car door, slid inside, and began entering the names into a portable computer. "You're a curious kid, aren't you?"

"Not usually," Teddy replied.

"I don't know what to make of you, Teddy," Barnes

continued as he tapped away on the computer. "You're new in town, you seem nice, but both times I've run into you, you've been involved in something . . . odd." He finished typing. "Okay, here's Eugene Sloot. Old case—not much on him."

"He went up the tree next door and never came down," Teddy said.

"Wow. You're right about it being next door. But it says his father reported that he ran away."

"Maybe that's where he ran."

"It's not likely he's been up there for sixty years. Tell me more about Albert Barker," Barnes said, clicking the computer to another screen.

"He went into the river."

Barnes pulled up computer images of Albert's old file. "Whoa. Sorry, Teddy. It says Albert was at a movie the day he vanished. He disappeared from the Uptown Theater."

"No, he didn't. He went to the river on his bike."

"I just pulled the old report. His mother told police he would never have missed that movie—he went to see it the first day it came out."

"*The Empire Strikes Back?*" Teddy asked.

Barnes looked at Teddy and raised an eyebrow. "That's right. How'd you know?"

"He loved *Star Wars*, and *Empire Strikes Back* came out in 1980, the year he disappeared."

"That doesn't explain why he'd be at the river."

"He might miss a movie if he got chased off by bullies," Teddy continued. "Were there any witnesses that saw him *inside* the theater that day?"

Barnes carefully jotted down notes in his book as Teddy spoke. "The river, eh? They never checked down there."

"Maybe that's why they didn't find him," Teddy said.

"Okay, then. Why would he be *in* the river?"

"What if the bully followed him and he got scared? And what if he jumped in to get away because maybe a bully wouldn't follow him into the water?"

"That's a lot of 'what ifs' and 'maybes.' You got a name for your theoretical bully?" Barnes held his pen ready.

Teddy hesitated. He couldn't say it. Barnes already suspected he'd broken into Mulligan's trailer, and he probably didn't need much more to make an arrest. "You don't believe any of this anyway," Teddy said.

Barnes looked Teddy straight in the eye. "Help me believe, Teddy."

"Did you notice that those boys were all twelve and disappeared exactly at the end of a decade?"

Barnes turned back to his computer and checked the screen, then double-checked as he scratched his chin in thought. "Nobody has ever connected these disappearances. What are you onto here?"

"I don't know," Teddy sighed.

"Neither do I. Kids go missing all the time, and it's probably nothing more than an extremely disturbing coincidence. But I'm interested. What else can you tell me?"

"I can tell you that I'm twelve, and it's the end of the decade right now."

"I see," Barnes said. "Anything else?"

Teddy thought hard. It was tempting to keep talking, to tell Barnes everything, but what could he say? That he stole a knife from the bully he'd hit with a rock thirty years ago? That a tree tried to devour him?

He glanced at the sycamore above them, suddenly afraid that it was listening. "No," he mumbled.

"Tell you what," Barnes said as he leaned out of the car to hand Teddy a business card. "I'm going to go do some more poking around. If you think of anything else, anything at all, don't hesitate to call my cell phone, instead of nine-one-one, okay?"

"Okay.

"And whatever you do, stay out of other people's houses."

But Teddy wasn't listening anymore. *Mulligan's house was where I found all of the clues*, he realized. He looked past the sycamore at the A-house, then back at the tree. It almost seemed like the tree was standing guard. *Like it wants to keep me away from the house*, he thought.

"Teddy?" Barnes said, snapping his fingers. "Did you hear me?"

"Right," Teddy said, nodding and giving Barnes the fake smile he'd learned from his mother. "Stay out of other houses."

CHAPTER 16

Once his mom went to bed that night, Teddy snuck out the front door with a backpack full of equipment for his journey into the A-house.

Mulligan's knife was still in his pocket, while his pack held the hatchet and weed killer from the garage and a crowbar to pry his way into the A-house. He packed a portable 500-watt halogen light capable of illuminating entire rooms in the dark home, and, to be safe, a smaller flashlight. A compass and a cell phone seemed like good ideas too, as did a few granola bars. Finally, Teddy threw in a long rope—

he hadn't forgotten his harrowing fall from the tall tree.

Before he left, he pinned a note to his pillow for his mom. It said not to worry and that he'd be back "later."

Feeling prepared, Teddy looked across the fence at the front door of the abandoned A-house. The dirty glass of the rusty fixture above the door was glowing yellowish-white as though the light had been turned on to welcome a visitor.

Weird, Teddy thought. *The bulb must be sixty years old, and the place can't possibly have electricity.*

He took a deep breath. He would rather have waited until morning, but he felt like time was running out. So he crept across the A-house yard, circling around the tree as far from the trunk as possible, and stepped up to the front door.

He knew he'd have to be careful not to leave signs of a break-in, whether he found more answers or not, so he covered his hand with his T-shirt to avoid leaving fingerprints and checked the knob. He was a little surprised to find it unlocked, yet relieved—at least he wouldn't have to use the crowbar.

Teddy pulled against the drift of sand on the porch and eased the door open. It was dark inside the boarded-up home, so he removed the halogen lamp from his pack. The lamp had a heavy battery, which Teddy detached and put in his pack so he could hold the light more easily. A cord plugged into the handle kept the battery connected.

But before he could flip the power switch, the light in the hall ahead of him came on with a quiet *click*. At the same time, the porch light winked off behind him.

It wants me to visit, he remembered thinking the day he'd arrived and come to the A-house porch.

The instinct to flee was strong—to run home, tuck himself in his bed and bury his fear under the safety of his comforter. Teddy looked back at his own house.

But isn't that exactly what the tree would have me do? he thought. *Is it guarding the A-house's secrets?* He reminded himself that he would never know if he ran, so he stepped inside.

Moving across the foyer, he found himself in a furnished living room containing an ancient scroll-armed couch that had collapsed in the middle and a dull, insect-eaten coffee table. Through an archway he saw a rusty dinette set with green chairs whose plastic upholstery had dried and split with age.

It seemed to Teddy that the owners had abandoned the place in a hurry, leaving all of their furniture, and that no one had set foot inside since. The air smelled stale, like the corpse of the cat he'd once found in an old shed long after it had withered to leather.

He continued down the main hall, each footstep leaving a print in the decades of dust on the floor. Despite the decay, the lights overhead turned on ahead of him and off behind him as he passed, leading him to a door with a couple of faded old baseball cards thumbtacked to it.

The players were unfamiliar—Dixie Walker and Elmer Riddle of the Pittsburgh Pirates. Teddy unpinned one and turned it over—the season was listed as 1948, a year when Sloot would have been alive.

There will be secrets and clues inside this room, Teddy thought. But it took a moment to bring himself to turn the knob, and when he did, his hand shook. Finally, he pushed the door open. It squeaked as if to announce his arrival.

A night lamp blinked on beside a small bed as the light in the hall abandoned him. In its glow, Teddy could see a dusty jar of marbles on the dresser. A mildew-stained wooden toy tank aimed up at him from the floor, and an old tabletop hockey game with worn metal players sat on the shelf.

Teddy crossed to the closet and peeked inside. It was full of crumbling, moth-eaten clothes sized for a kid his age. A pair of black and white Chuck Taylors sat decaying on a shelf, and two rusted metal baseball cleats hung from a hook near the top of the wall.

It was then that Teddy saw the small trapdoor in the ceiling. At first he almost ignored it, but then he noticed it was slightly open.

Just as the sycamore tree had invited him to climb it, Teddy now felt himself strangely drawn to the little door, as though it was open for a reason. People kept secrets in attics—*look up here*, it seemed to say.

He climbed up on the shelf and lifted the trapdoor enough to poke his head through. The attic was dark, so Teddy clicked on his light and swung the halogen's beam across the room.

The attic seemed to run the length of the house. There

was no proper floor—only rows of beams nailed on top of the ceiling below. Teddy lifted himself completely into the room for a closer look.

Then he saw the branches.

They wove between the beams in the rafters, crisscrossing and filling the attic like a huge, tangled vine. Shining the light along the walls, Teddy saw that they'd come in through the broken window at the end of the room, then spread throughout the entire attic.

The sprawling limbs told him that he'd come to the right place. The tree was here, and it was protecting something. He stepped out onto the beam, but he was still staring ahead, and that's when his foot slipped off.

As Teddy fell, his shorts ripped, and he felt something sharp tear into his leg. He landed hard, straddling the beams and grabbed his thigh. Warm stickiness ran through his fingers.

Blood!

He turned the light on his leg. There was *a lot* of blood. It ran over his knee in a steady stream so that his upper leg looked like someone had painted it solid red. Jammed into the torn flesh of his wound was the sharp point of a thick branch.

It suddenly felt stiflingly hot in the attic. Teddy swayed and sucked for breath, his head swimming. He turned on his stomach to crawl for the trapdoor, but it was too late. Before he could reach it, he passed out.

CHAPTER 17

Teddy awoke groggily to the sound of a window squealing open in the room below him. He retrieved the halogen lamp and shined it ahead, pulling himself to the trapdoor, where he scrambled through and dropped back into the closet.

When he landed, he remembered that his leg was injured. But when he looked down, he saw that it was no longer bleeding. Frantically, he pulled his shorts aside—there was now no wound at all.

He frowned, wondering if he'd just imagined the ill-fated trip to the attic the same way he might have imagined the scrub-brush park and the construction site. But if he had, his imagination was still at work, for the bedroom now appeared completely different than it had before.

The clothes hanging around him in the closet were no longer old and decayed but neat and pressed. Across the room, the cat-eye marbles were clean and sparkled in their jar, and the hockey game looked shiny new, as though waiting to be played with. In fact, the room appeared just as it might have in 1950.

Cautiously, Teddy stepped out of the closet and walked over to the bed. He felt the kid-sized indentation in the sheets on the bed and was surprised to find it warm. Someone had just gotten out of bed.

As Teddy stood by the bed, a hand reached through the open window by the headboard and pushed the drapes aside. Teddy turned to see a familiar face appear in the window frame.

"Sloot!" Teddy exclaimed. "I found you!"

"I was about to say the same thing, bucko." Sloot grinned back at him.

"Okay," Teddy said, "let's get you in here."

"No, let's get *you* in *here*," Sloot shot back. "If my dad catches you in my room . . . well, he's a bit of a hothead, I'll tell ya. I ain't supposed to have friends over at night. C'mon, let's scram. We can hole up in the tree." Sloot motioned for Teddy to come to the window, then ducked out of view.

"Wait," Teddy called. He stepped to the window frame and stuck his head through. The swirling darkness outside made it impossible to see. He was just about to point the halogen lamp out the window when a half-dozen hands grabbed him and yanked him through.

CHAPTER 18

Teddy fell to the ground. He could only see vague shapes in the dark, and a strong wind was blowing sand in his eyes. He felt flailing limbs and bodies around him, wrestling him to the ground. He thrashed and struck out in all directions with his fists and feet. He felt one punch connect with something solid—flesh and bone. Then a body leaped on him and pinned him down.

"Sloot! Help!" he yelled. But no help came. Sloot had left the window moments before the hands pulled Teddy through, but now he was gone.

It occurred to Teddy that perhaps the police had come

and they were the ones holding him down. Maybe they'd grabbed Sloot too, or he'd run away from them. Then he had a scarier thought—it might be Henry Mulligan and his hoodlum friends.

Teddy felt himself being lifted and carried. He still couldn't make out the figures, and he couldn't keep track of which way they were taking him. Not that it really mattered—he'd lost all sense of direction in the struggle.

Don't panic, he told himself.

With great effort, he stopped himself from squirming and tried to think. By the number of hands on him, he judged that there were three, maybe four of them. Police would have identified themselves, he thought, so it probably wasn't cops. But whoever had him wasn't talking, so he'd have to wait to figure anything else out.

He didn't have to wait long. They were half dragging him now, and the halogen lamp was dangling by its cord behind him. The lamp caught on something in the dark, and it jerked the battery in Teddy's backpack, which tightened the straps on his shoulders and yanked him free of their grasp.

Teddy fell to the ground and immediately scrambled

away from the group. He heard their footsteps shuffling around in confusion, and he desperately fumbled along the ground in the dark for the light. He found the halogen and, holding it out like a shield, he flicked on the switch.

Five hundred watts of light suddenly blew the darkness back. The glare hurt his eyes, and he was blinded for a moment. He heard eerie squeals of pain, commotion, and panicked footsteps. When his eyes adjusted, whoever had attacked him had retreated beyond the lamp's range into the darkness and dust. But he knew they were still out there beyond the dim edge of the light's reach.

"Teddy, wait!" It was Sloot's voice.

"Sloot!" Teddy called out. "Over here! Quick. They're all around us." He swung the light back and forth, expecting Henry Mulligan to leap out and grab him at any second.

"Lower the lamp," Sloot called. "It burns our peepers, pal."

"Our?" Teddy turned the lamp toward the ground so that it cast only a faint circle of light, enough to see by, but not so bright.

Two pale eyes appeared in the blackness. Sloot melted from the shadows and eased toward him, squinting. "This is a dim place," he said, rubbing his eyes.

"What does that mean?" Teddy asked. But before Sloot could answer, he heard footsteps to his left. "Watch out!" he warned, and he raised the light.

Sloot stepped to him, squinting in the halogen's blinding beam, and pushed the light back down toward the ground. "Stop, Teddy," he pleaded. "It's us."

Sloot motioned to the darkness, beckoning forward his unseen companions. A second boy crept from the shadows, then a third. They were pale and hollow-eyed. The third one had a bloody nose. They were about Teddy's age, and he was relieved to see that none were Henry Mulligan or from his gang.

Sloot patted them on their backs as they joined him and Teddy in the faint light. "Joey and Oliver, this is Teddy. He's here to help us."

Teddy gasped. "The other boys from the cemetery!"

CHAPTER 19

Joey and Oliver nodded, but didn't speak. Joey fidgeted, while Oliver wiped blood from his nose with his shirtsleeve.

"Not too chatty, I'm afraid," Sloot said. "But they're very glad you've finally come here, believe me."

He smiled. It was an odd, crooked smile.

"But where is here?" Teddy swung the halogen around. All he could see was blowing sand in all directions. He'd been taken too far from the A-house to see the old home in the darkness.

"Halfway between," Sloot said. "Not bright like life, not black like death. Just . . . dim."

Teddy didn't push it. By now he cared less about where he was than about how to get out. But whatever was after him had clearly brought the other boys to this place. Maybe they could tell him what it was if they could all get to some-place safe to talk.

"Where are Albert and Walter," Teddy asked, "and the last one? It's Lawrence, right?"

Joey and Oliver looked at each other. They murmured as though they knew something.

Sloot waved the boys silent. "Lawrence is in the tree. We weren't sure you'd be coming."

Teddy checked the dangling cord from the halogen to his backpack to make sure it wouldn't catch on anything again.

"Seriously, we should all go," he said. "But I don't want to leave without everyone. And who were those dark people that attacked me? Was it Henry Mulligan and his friends?"

The boys shot furtive looks at one another again. It made Teddy nervous.

"Servants of the tree," Sloot answered finally.

As he spoke, a low, loud groan rose behind Teddy. Sloot glanced upward, looking fearful and angry at once.

"He's here, isn't he?" Sloot shouted up into the swirling dust and darkness.

The hairs on the back of Teddy's neck stood on end. He pointed the halogen up to the sky, revealing a massive shadow, which towered over them.

It was the tree.

CHAPTER 20

The sycamore was so big that Teddy had simply mistaken it for a wall of darkness. But now it was revealed by the light in all of its horrible glory. The ragged trunk twisted skyward, more than fifteen feet wide. Its thick bark was crusty and cracked with open scars that oozed inky sap. Overhead, gnarled branches jutted in all directions, their tips well beyond the reach of Teddy's light. Its deep bass groans echoed in the blackness and shook the ground.

The boys ducked out of the spotlight, and Teddy backed away, trying to protect them with the lamp.

"Take the light off it," Sloot warned. "You're making it angry."

Before Teddy could respond, he heard a softer moaning from above. He moved the light to the left, and, to his horror, he saw a body hanging in lower limbs of the tree.

It was a tall boy he didn't recognize, but since it wasn't Albert or Walter, he had a chilling idea who it might be. "Is that Lawrence?" he gasped.

Sloot nodded, unsurprised.

The clawlike branches cradled Lawrence, holding him in place while writhing leaves plastered his body like leeches seeming to suck out his energy the way a normal leaf might suck in the sun. The leaves shrank from Teddy's beam, however, then popped off of Lawrence's skin, leaving hideous red welts. Teddy continued to shine the light on the tree, and the branches themselves retreated, releasing Lawrence. The tall boy plummeted to the ground.

Without thinking, Teddy darted forward to drag Lawrence out of reach. He kept the light pointed up at the grotesque tree to keep the branches at bay.

As he pulled Lawrence away, Teddy turned to Sloot. "It uses you as . . . fertilizer?" he sputtered.

"Ah, you get it," Sloot said. "It's so much better when we

don't have to explain it, like we do with stupid kids." He glanced at Oliver. "There's not much light for it here in the dimness, you see. It needs energy, and we've got it. As long as there's a new source provided every ten years or so, no one has to get completely drained. We take turns."

"What?" Teddy yelped. He began to back away from both the tree and the boys as the weirdness of the past three days became suddenly, terrifyingly clear. The snags waiting for Albert in the river, the roots that grabbed Walter in the sewer trench, the knothole that held Sloot like a puppet. The tree wasn't stalking the dead boys—it already had them. And it was using them to lure a new victim . . . him.

But Teddy hadn't gone in the river, the trench, or the knothole. *I never took the bait*, he realized.

The thought gave him hope. Holding out the light, he spoke more bravely than he felt. "You're not gonna feed me to some plant!"

"It's not a choice," Sloot said. "You're already here."

"No way!" Teddy insisted. "It hates light, and I've got five hundred watts of tree-repellant power right in my hands."

"Yeah," Sloot said, "that's a bit of a problem."

He motioned to Joey, who pulled out a well-worn Cub Scout pocketknife and grabbed the halogen's cord.

"Wait!" Teddy cried, but it was too late.

Joey cut the cord, plunging them all into dimness and swirling dust.

CHAPTER 21

Teddy ran blindly. The grainy wind stung his eyes, and the deep sand pulled at his feet. He felt sure the boys were about to catch him, but then he heard Sloot yell from a distance behind him. "Let him go. The desert will send him back. He'll *want* to come back."

Teddy tried to run straight to keep some sense of direction in the blowing dust. He sprinted until his breath came in gasps and his lungs hurt. When he finally felt he was far enough from the tree and the boys, he slowed to a trot so he could think.

Maybe he could circle back to the house. It was how he'd gotten here—through the window.

It has to lead back out, doesn't it?

As he jogged, the sand gave way to a crunchy surface like gravel, but softer. He still couldn't see well in the dimness, so he slowed to a walk for fear of running headlong into something solid. He reached into his backpack for the small flashlight he'd packed. It was no 500-watt halogen, and the batteries wouldn't last forever, but it was better than nothing.

He clicked on the flashlight and shined it ahead— nothing but darkness as far as he could see. At least there were no trees or double-crossing kids. A wave of relief washed over him and for a moment he relaxed, at least until he pointed the light down.

In the bright beam, he could see the ground moving. Teddy gasped—it was an undulating carpet of bugs, all waving oversized pincers and upturned tails.

Scorpions!

He swung the flashlight in a full circle around him, scanning the heaving swarm of poisonous creatures. There were thousands of them, and he'd run directly into their midst. He took a tentative step back, and his heel made a loud crunch. Scorpions skittered away in every direction.

No more than a bee sting, he told himself, trying to stay calm. *But what would a thousand stings do to me?*

The scorpions were now scuttling across his tennis shoes as the throng closed in again around his motionless feet. At first, Teddy tried to delicately tiptoe into the open spaces between the horrible little creatures. But they kept crawling toward him, flooding the desert floor and filling every gap. So Teddy began to trot again, crunching with every step, high-stepping like a football player running through tires at practice.

His legs pistoned up and down, feet smashing scorpions into bits of shell and white jelly with every step, but they never touched the ground long enough for his tormentors to climb aboard. It was exhausting—he was already tired from fleeing the boys, and he knew he couldn't stop or the scorpions would swarm over him in an instant.

But because he tried to keep the flashlight pointed straight ahead to see where he was going, he couldn't look down, and when the ground suddenly dropped away, he toppled into a hole.

CHAPTER 22

The flashlight flew from his hand, its beam waving uselessly in random directions as Teddy plummeted for anxious seconds. It was just long enough to wonder if he was falling to his death, but then he hit the ground. Hard.

Teddy rolled over, groaning in agony. His left knee was throbbing—he'd twisted it in an awkward direction when he landed—but he desperately crawled for the flashlight, which had landed a few feet away. The horror of losing the light was stronger than the pain.

Luckily, he didn't feel anything crawl over his bare hand as he reached along the ground. And when he grabbed the light and shined it around, he was relieved to see that he'd fallen clear of the scorpions.

Teddy got to his feet, favoring his knee, and looked around to see where he'd landed. He found himself in a trench that was about five feet wide, with walls that rose straight up on either side of him—ten tall feet of dirt, rocks, and sinewy tree roots.

There was no way he could reach the top, and he didn't dare grab hold of the roots to climb—he certainly didn't trust them. But it didn't matter—a scorpion dropped over the edge of the trench, falling at his feet, and he suddenly didn't want to go up anyway.

As if on cue, dozens more scorpions began to pour into the trench after the first one, dropping to the ground behind Teddy. The path was clear the other way, so he turned around and limped away as fast as he could in that direction.

Even slowed by his injured leg, he outdistanced the scorpions. But if he paused to rest, even for a second, they quickly began to gather behind him again. So he continued along the trench with the unpleasant feeling that the creeping little things were herding him onward.

As Teddy limped along, he began to notice a squishing sound with each footfall. Looking down, he saw that a trickle of brownish sludge was now running along the ground, and the air started to smell foul, like an outhouse.

This is a sewer trench, he realized. He started to feel nauseated and picked up the pace, hoping to find a way out of the trench.

Just then, Teddy began to hear a banging sound, and he came to a wooden ladder hanging down the wall to his left.

Upon closer inspection, the ladder seemed to be made of entwined roots, but they did not appear to be a random tangle—there were distinct rungs leading up to the top of the trench.

Meanwhile, the banging continued somewhere above him. It sounded like a hammer frantically smacking a nail.

Teddy hesitated, unsure what to do. He was suspicious of the tree-root ladder, even with the scorpions still trailing him, but the smell was getting worse, and the trickle at his feet had grown now to a steady stream.

All at once, the hammering grew much louder and even wilder. The scorpions scattered to both sides of the trench, fleeing up the walls.

"Uh-oh," Teddy said.

There was a low rumble, and he whipped the flashlight around, illuminating a huge wall of sewage barreling down the trench toward him.

Teddy leaped onto the root ladder and climbed like mad for the top of the trench as the wave roared past beneath him. The murky filth kept rising as he made his way up and each rung began to unravel beneath his foot as soon as he stepped on it.

Up and up he climbed as the rungs dissolved, and with a great heave, he pulled himself up over the edge just as the sewage crested the top of the trench.

Teddy crawled along the trench's edge, half-expecting to find himself in the middle of a sea of scorpions again. But they were gone. He was also surprised to find that he could see without the flashlight. It was dim, and there was no sign of a sun, but enough light was filtering through the blowing dust that he could shut the flashlight off and save the batteries.

Before him, the skeleton of a half-built home rose from the sand. But it looked all wrong.

The frame of the house was horribly distorted. Warped two-by-four boards curved up every few feet, arching into the air like a dead dinosaur's rib cage. A crooked staircase rose in one direction, then turned and came back down without ever reaching the next floor. And because the walls were not yet filled in, it was impossible to tell where rooms began and ended. A tilted porch jutted out from the front of the home like a lolling tongue.

Atop it all, perched on the cockeyed, unfinished archway over the porch, sat Walter. He grinned down at Teddy.

"Scaredy! You made it."

CHAPTER 23

Walter twirled a massive hammer as if it were a cheerleader's baton. Like the house, the hammer looked like something from a twisted cartoon—its narrow handle led to a mallet-shaped head the size of a cantaloupe. But when Walter fumbled and dropped it, it hit the porch floor with a very real crash. It splintered the wood, leaving a gaping hole.

"Whoops," Walter said with a smirk.

The hammer gone, he hoisted a circular saw with jagged three-inch teeth and a long cord that trailed away to nowhere. He pulled the trigger and it roared to life, seemingly without any power source. Walter haphazardly sliced through a board next to him, and it fell away, punching another hole through the porch.

"Watch out!" Teddy called.

"Or what?" Walter said. "This?" He revved up the saw again and, without flinching, whacked off one of his own fingers.

"Walter!" Teddy gasped. "Your finger! It's . . ."

"What?" Walter shrugged. "C'mon, Scaredy, spit it out."

"Don't you see? You . . . you cut it off!"

"Uh-oh," he said, chuckling and inspecting the empty space above the stump of his newly missing left index finger. "Same thing happened the day I came here, you know."

There should have been blood—plenty of blood—but there wasn't, and Walter didn't seem any worse off with one less finger. Teddy had to take a deep breath to calm himself.

"Where is here?"

"Don't you recognize it?" Walter said. "This is my *place*. Everybody here has a place, Teddy. You will too."

Teddy shivered. "So I didn't just imagine the construction site from 1970," he said. "I was *there*."

Walter laughed. "Wasn't that fun?"

"You tried to lure me here that day," Teddy said, suddenly angry. "You tried to get me to come to this awful place the same way you got here—through the sewer trench!"

"Awww, I thought we were pals."

"You're not my friend," Teddy said, as much to himself as to Walter.

"It's not just me," Walter said. "Good ol' Sloot gave it a try too. Even your big-bellied buddy was working on you."

"Albert?" Teddy breathed.

"Oh-ho-ho! I can't believe you're so naïve. He's the one who picked you out! I laughed my buns off watching him try to coax you into the river."

Teddy glared upward, wondering how he could have been so stupid.

"C'mon, don't be mad," Walter cooed. "We just want more friends."

"So why didn't you stay?" Teddy said. "Something grabbed you in the trench."

"My turn was up. You see, a new kid like you can visit our time at the place we crossed over, but you can only see what happened to each of us once, and only for a few minutes. Enough time for us to try to convince you to come over too. But nobody could get you to take the leap. Too chicken, I guess. Bawk-bawk-buh-kawwwwk!"

"Too smart," Teddy said.

"So smart that you came here on your own?" Walter chided him. "Welcome."

He revved up the saw again and cut through the wooden archway on which he was sitting. The entire arch collapsed and he fell to the porch, landing on his feet.

"Tah-dah!" Walter said, raising his arms in the air like an Olympic gymnast after a big dismount. "Enough chit-chat. I'm supposed to bring you to the tree."

He started toward Teddy with the toothy saw still clenched in one fist. Teddy backed away, wondering how he could fight someone who could cut off his own finger without feeling any pain.

Then he realized that Walter's finger had been gone since 1970. *That was only a replay.* But there was the punch Teddy had thrown in the dark when Sloot, Joey, and Oliver had jumped him. *I gave Oliver that bloody nose*, he thought. *The boys can be hurt here.*

As he backed up, his foot felt the edge of the trench. It

gave him an idea. Teddy waved his arms, pretending like he was fighting for balance to keep from falling in.

"Where you going?" Walter taunted. "Back into the sewer? Ick." He charged at Teddy, the circular saw roaring, its cord dangling between Walter's legs.

"No," Teddy snapped, suddenly crouching, more balanced and ready than he'd let on. "You are!"

In one swift motion, he dove and grabbed the saw's cord, yanking it taut between Walter's legs. Walter's foot hooked the cord, and he stumbled, plummeting into the sewer trench.

There was a sickening *crack* as Walter hit the floor of the trench, where the sludge had drained away. All was silent for a moment, but then Teddy heard something even more gut-wrenching—Walter's pleading voice.

He was no longer laughing. In fact, it sounded to Teddy like he was crying.

"Hellllp!" Walter begged. "I think my leg's broken. Please. I can't climb up—I hurt my finger. There's scorpions down here. I wanna go home."

It was hard to listen. Teddy realized that Walter's pleas were what he must have said in 1970 on the day he disappeared—the dim world was replaying his disappearance.

But as sad as Walter's cries made him feel, Teddy knew he couldn't let him out. He was far too dangerous.

"I'll look for you when I get free," he called down.

"I'm scared," came Walter's shaky voice from below.

"I promise," Teddy said, then he turned and walked away from the skeletal construction site.

As Teddy left, the frame of the house began to collapse, its timbers cracking like matchsticks and falling like dominoes. There was a series of tremendous crashes, then a strong wind carried in the desert sand to finish burying Walter completely.

CHAPTER 24

It somehow seemed inevitable that Walter would be buried in this world as he had been in life, Teddy thought as he trudged on through the drifting sand. But he still felt the loss as strongly as he had the first time, and he had to force himself to concentrate on his own dire circumstances.

He hoped that the layout of the dim world mirrored that of the real Richland, even in a rough, bizarre way. If it did, he was walking in the general direction of the river from the construction site. And if he found the river, he could use it to locate the A-house again.

With no scorpions or dead boys chasing him, Teddy stopped for a moment to rummage through his backpack and see what else he had that might help. His compass didn't work, and the cell phone he'd packed blinked "no service." It didn't surprise him, and besides, even if he got hold of someone, he could never explain where he was.

He ate a granola bar and walked on, watching ahead for the river. This version of Richland was an empty place. There didn't seem to be anything but desert wasteland between the A-house, Walter's construction site, and where he hoped to find the river.

As he walked, he puzzled over what Walter had said—how they each had a place here in this world. *If the construction site was Walter's,* Teddy thought, *then the river must be Albert's.* He wondered where his own might be.

After a few minutes, Teddy's theory of the river's location proved correct—the great waterway appeared in the distance like a ribbon of ink winding through the sand. Darkness rolled off of its surface like mist, casting shadows along the bank. *It's glowing black,* Teddy thought—the exact opposite of a river reflecting sunlight from its surface.

Drawing closer, he saw that the bare, sandy dirt gave way to gray, scrubby plants along the pebbly shore. Teddy stooped and picked up a rock—a potent weapon against other kids. Albert had seemed like the most harmless of the three boys, but perhaps it made him the most dangerous too.

"Albert?" he called. There was no response. The river just flowed past, eerily quiet for something so huge.

Teddy looked up and down the lonely bank, but there was no sign of the chubby boy. He hurled the rock into the water. The current quickly swept the ripples downstream, but Teddy saw a shape linger just beneath the surface. It was moving, but Teddy couldn't tell what it was.

The shape in the water began to grow—it was coming closer. Teddy saw what looked like an arm, long and thin. He could almost make out a bony hand.

"Albert?"

He set one foot near the edge of the bank for a better look. The river crawled up the shore toward him and flowed over his foot. Teddy felt its current tug at his pant leg.

Suddenly, a large figure burst from the water. It slammed

full-force into Teddy and knocked him backward onto the sand-and-stone bank, landing directly on top of him.

Teddy groaned and stared up into a familiar dripping face.

"Don't go in the river," Albert warned.

CHAPTER 25

"Okay," Teddy wheezed, after his heart stopped pounding. "Stay out of the water. I get it."

"What the heck are you doing here?" Albert whispered.

"I was looking for you!" Teddy blurted out, squirming beneath Albert's weight.

"Shhh," Albert warned. "Keep it down."

"What were *you* doing in the water?" Teddy asked loudly.

"Shhh . . . as in, shut up," Albert said. "They'll hear you."

Teddy rolled Albert off of him, and not too gently. "Who will?"

Albert cast his guilty eyes downward. "The ones who want you to stay."

"You and your buddies, right?"

"Richland isn't all sun," Albert continued. "There's another side. A dark side."

"And you're part of it," Teddy said, jabbing the chubby boy in the chest. Suddenly, he was furious with Albert. "You're a fat, dead, stinking liar!"

Albert sighed. "I'm not totally dead."

"Almost dead, then. Whatever. You tried to lure me into the water. You picked me out."

"I didn't have a choice. But I tried to warn you."

"Warn me?"

"I told you to bike away and forget me."

"That's not a warning," Teddy snapped. "'Hey, look out, I'm not just a chunky *Star Wars* fan, I'm dead. And I'm trying to make you dead too.' *That's* a warning."

"I'm not dead," Albert insisted.

"You disappeared in the river. They never found you. That sounds like dead to me."

Albert looked away, staring out across the water. After a while, he spoke, as much to himself as to Teddy. "I live it over and over, but I never quite get dead. The bullies come, I go into the river, my feet get tangled in sunken branches, and I show up here."

It was hard to be mad at someone who had to die over and over. It sounded lonely and sad. "So the branches grab you?" Teddy asked softly.

"They still have me. I can't get loose." Albert grew quiet, and Teddy put a comforting hand on his shoulder.

They stood on the shore in silence for a moment until Teddy felt the wind change direction. He looked up and saw a wall of swirling sand blotting out the sky, a tan curtain sweeping toward them.

"What's that?" Teddy gasped.

"Sandstorm," Albert said. "You've gotta get out of here."

Upstream, Teddy saw shadowy dunes rising from the bank of the river like a wall. Tumbleweeds taller than himself began to bounce past, threatening to knock them into the water.

"We're wasting time," Albert said, his tone suddenly more serious than Teddy had ever heard it before. "The tree is near, and the others are coming. You're fresh, full of life. It can feed on you for a long time before we have to start taking turns feeding it again. You've got to get away before they find you."

"Away where?"

Albert pointed straight into the teeth of the swirling dust. "Back through the storm."

"I'm not going *into* it."

Albert frowned. "Look, I feel bad that you're here. I really didn't mean it. I want you to go back and have a life."

As Teddy debated what to do, the long, thin arm he'd seen before in the water slithered toward the shore, groping for them. Teddy now saw that it was not an arm, but a gnarled, clawlike branch.

"Look out!" he said.

"Yep, it's coming," Albert said without looking toward the shore. "And I'm gonna catch it for this. Go. Don't turn around. Don't stop."

"But go where? How do I get out?"

"I dunno. Where you came in, maybe?"

"Come with me," Teddy pleaded.

Albert smiled. "You go. This time *I'll* try to hold them off, buddy." He stooped and picked up a rock. "You're almost out of time," Albert said, watching the branch in the river out of the corner of his eye.

"I'm staying," Teddy said defiantly.

Albert threw the rock. It sailed into the water and hit the branch.

Teddy cringed as he saw the branch writhe, at first curling up like an injured snake, then exposing more of its length, twisting up from under the water. It was huge, and there were more arms than just the one that crawled to the shore.

"A few seconds," Albert said. "That's all the time I can buy you."

Watching the water churn, Teddy saw dozens of grasping wooden claws erupt from the surface of the river. They stretched out like tentacles, reaching for him and Albert.

Teddy turned to flee, grabbing Albert to drag him along. At first he thought Albert was resisting him, but then he saw that his companion was actually being pulled into the river by the spindly wooden hands. Within seconds, his feet and thick calves were submerged.

"I don't want you to see this," Albert moaned.

As Albert slid into the water, the skin on his arms and

legs began to contort and bloat. His face turned purple as the woody fingers of the serpentine branches slid up over his shoulders to pull him down. He fought to keep his head above the water, but it didn't matter—he was drowning before Teddy's eyes, just as he had thirty years ago.

A wet gurgle erupted from his swollen mouth.

"Go-oooo!"

Horrified, Teddy turned and ran.

CHAPTER 26

As Teddy fought his way through the wind, he felt a dull ache in the pit of his stomach. Watching Albert drown was perhaps the worst thing he'd ever seen. He felt awful leaving him, and he had to remind himself that the chubby boy was part of the reason he was here. Still, the image of his swollen face replayed in his head, over and over.

But Albert was gone, and Teddy again forced himself to focus on his own escape. If his theory was correct that the geography here mirrored Richland, the A-house and the window back to the real world would be downriver from Walter's construction site and inland less than a mile.

But the sandstorm was growing stronger, pushing him sideways as he trudged on. He tasted grit on his tongue and felt it in his ears.

After a few minutes in the blinding dust, he wasn't sure he was going straight anymore. With nothing in sight for reference, he wondered if he was actually wandering farther from the window rather than closer. He was also getting tired.

He stopped for a moment and shielded his eyes from the hot, stinging sand. He desperately needed to rest and gather his strength. But as he stood there, a huge tumbleweed broadsided him, lashing his skin with thorns and tossing him head over heels.

He landed flat on the ground, and sand immediately began pouring over his face and limbs as though it was trying to bury him. Teddy fought to his knees and crawled forward, feeling for any kind of protection from the howling wind and sand.

It seemed hopeless until Teddy felt a hard, downward-sloping surface beneath him. He scooted forward and slid down into a concrete ditch about two feet deep with a flat bottom.

Thankfully, he was out of the wind, and the dust seemed to be mostly blowing over the top of the ditch. But his legs still ached from fighting through the sand, and he was tired from constantly running away from the horrors of the dim world. He started to lie down, hoping to rest for a few minutes.

"Don't do that here," a voice said.

Through the gusting sand at the edge of the ditch above him, Teddy saw a vague face. "Who's there?" he asked.

"It's me."

"Me who?"

"Lawrence," the face said, and a large hand reached down to Teddy from out of the storm. "I gotta take you back to the tree," he said matter-of-factly.

"No way," Teddy replied. "You'll have to drag me there."

"I know you're hot and tired," Lawrence said, leaning down toward Teddy. "Your muscles are sore. You want to lie down and rest. Just for a minute, you're telling yourself. But you won't get up. The sand is already covering you."

It was eerie how Lawrence knew what he was thinking. And the sand *was* inching over his shoes again. Teddy struggled to his weary feet, swaying in the ditch. "I can still walk."

"You'll never find your way out of the desert." There was no mocking or irony in his voice. In fact, he sounded emotionless to Teddy, like a weary robot. It was as though he had almost no energy at all.

"I'll take my chances," Teddy said.

"No. Look around you. The sand and wind will scour your flesh until all that's left of you is polished white bone. You don't want that."

Despite his brave statements, Teddy knew Lawrence was right. He was hopelessly lost. The hot wind still tore at his exposed skin, and he spat sand with every dry breath. He was sweating too, losing precious water.

"C'mon," Lawrence said. "This is a lonely spot to end up. Trust me. I know."

"This is *your* place," Teddy realized aloud.

Lawrence ignored the statement. "Come be with us now," he said.

Teddy reached out to Lawrence. The boy's hand was strangely cold in the hot air. *But you're all dead*, Teddy thought as Lawrence hauled him up out of the ditch.

"How did you end up out here?" he asked.

"I was hunting lizards when the dust storm hit," Lawrence said quietly, "way out past the gas station at the end of Saint Street. I fought my way back to here, but I didn't know how far I had to go, and it was so hot. I saw Sloot. Don't know how he got there, but he told me the ditch would give me shelter. He even got in first—said we'd walk out of the desert together when the storm passed. But once I got in the ditch, I never got out. I still wonder sometimes how far I had to go."

Lawrence looked out into the storm. "C'mon, let's get moving."

He led Teddy into the wind by the hand. Teddy stumbled along behind, too exhausted to argue.

They trudged in silence for a while before Teddy asked, "How do you know where we're going?"

"I've been here a long time," Lawrence said.

"It all looks the same to me," Teddy said.

"The wind always comes from the same direction."

"Where?"

"Everything radiates out from the tree," Lawrence explained, pointing ahead. "And you have to walk straight into a storm to get to its center."

CHAPTER 27

As they trudged along with their heads bowed in the wind, Teddy asked, "How did others get here, like Oliver?"

Lawrence didn't answer, but simply pointed ahead where a shadow rose in the dust. *The tree*, Teddy thought at first, but the shadow was too straight, too square.

They walked closer, and Teddy saw that it was a brick chimney with no house attached to it. Some of the bricks were missing, and tree roots ran through the holes. Others had partially crumbled from age. It towered into the air until Teddy could not see the top. At the bottom, a fireplace yawned open large enough for a boy to walk into.

Teddy stepped to it and ducked his head to look up the shaft.

"Don't go in," Lawrence warned. "Go around."

"Why?"

"This is where Oliver came through ten years ago."

"The chimney?"

"Yep. He was stuck in there. We heard him hollering when he arrived, and we had to come pull him out."

"You rescued him?"

"Well, we had to take him to the tree."

"Right. Of course." Teddy frowned and walked around the chimney. To his surprise, another chimney stood behind it. Yet another was visible in the dust beyond the second one.

He turned back around to face the first chimney and suddenly found himself in a forest of chimneys. There were brick walls behind him where the desert had been seconds earlier. In fact, he could see nothing *but* walls. He slid around a corner and walked a few paces, trying to backtrack, but he couldn't tell one wall from the next.

"Lawrence?" he called out, but there was no answer.

Teddy kept moving, but the chimneys were getting closer together. Some nearly touched each other, and he had to squeeze through the space between them.

"Lawrence? Somebody? Help!"

The walls were so close together now that they touched at the corners, and Teddy couldn't see between them anymore. He stood in a square, surrounded on four sides by the chimneys, and the only light he could see was a dim speck straight above him. It was almost like he was *inside* a single chimney, and the walls were still closing in.

Teddy felt the rough bricks wedge against his body, starting to squeeze him like a vise. The air smelled of old soot. Lawrence had led him into a trap—right into Oliver's personal nightmare.

The sycamore roots that wound through the holes in the brick tickled Teddy's bare skin, teasing him as if they were waiting for him to succumb. The tree didn't need to attack now—it could simply wait for him to die. He wondered how long it would take wedged in an old chimney. Hours? Days?

While Teddy waited for death to take him, something

small and black dropped in front of his face and dangled from a thin line. It stopped and swung back and forth in the narrow space between his head and the brick.

A *spider?* Teddy thought.

He squirmed as the spider rotated and slowly unfolded spindly legs, revealing a bright red hourglass-shaped mark on its belly.

A *black widow!*

The spider was only inches from him now. Teddy could see the twin fangs and the spinneret with which it would wrap up his face after it injected poison into him. He struggled against the bricks, scraping his elbows and knuckles, desperately trying to climb, but it was no use. He wondered if it would bite his nose, which was closest, or crawl up his cheek and sink its fangs into his eyeball.

As if in answer, the black widow launched itself and landed on his upper lip.

There was no more time to think. Teddy opened his mouth and sucked a sudden breath, pulling the spider straight in. Before the spider could react, he clamped his mouth shut, shoved it to one side with his tongue, and bit down.

Teddy felt the spider snap like a juicy kernel of corn be-tween his teeth. His stomach lurched, and he had to fight to keep from vomiting. But he felt no sting in his mouth. The horrid little thing hadn't been able to bite him first.

He spat the legs and runny remains of the spider's body against the brick in front of him, and when the queasy feel-ing began to pass, he grinned. He wasn't so helpless after all.

CHAPTER 28

Teddy's heart was still thumping hard when he felt a tug on his ankle. Then something grabbed both of his feet and yanked. He came unstuck from the chimney and slid down between the crushing walls, landing on his rump in a huge, open fireplace.

Lawrence dragged him out by the legs, dropping him in the sand. "I told you not to go in," he said.

"I didn't," Teddy gasped, bending at the waist and spitting more spider parts on the ground. "I went around."

"*All* the way around." Lawrence sighed in frustration. It was the first sign of emotion the zombielike boy had shown, as though being forced to help Teddy had given him some energy.

"You look a little queasy," Lawrence commented.

"Just something I ate." Teddy coughed.

Lawrence helped him up, and Teddy now saw where the forest of chimneys began and ended. They began to hike around the entire bunch, keeping well clear of even the chimneys on the outer edge to avoid being sucked in again.

"How did Oliver get stuck?" Teddy asked as they walked.

"His parents were at a church talking about getting divorced. I guess neither of them wanted to keep him. When he heard them arguing about who would have to take him, he hid up inside an old chimney in a boarded-up room the church didn't use anymore. Oliver said he didn't want them to find him, ever. Guess it worked."

"What about Joey?"

In response, Lawrence pointed ahead of them again.

Through the blowing dust, Teddy could see a huge wall coming into view. As they approached, he realized that it was made of intertwined roots, like a giant woven basket. It was high enough that the top of it faded into the dust over their heads, and it ran to their right and left until it disappeared in the distance, blocking their way completely.

"What's that?"

Lawrence pointed to the base of the wall, where a broken place in the roots revealed a black hole. "It's a crawl space."

"That's Joey's place?"

Lawrence nodded. "His dog liked to squeeze under a neighbor's house through a hole in the lattice. When it went missing for two days, Joey went looking for it. He never came home."

"He crawled under the house?"

"Yep."

"What happened to him?"

"We don't know. He won't talk about it. Doesn't talk much at all, really. He's a quiet kid anyway, and the tree drained him down pretty low as soon as he got here. It's getting hungrier, you know."

"No, I didn't know, actually," Teddy said. "All of this getting eaten by a plant stuff is new to me."

"Oh, yeah, right. Sorry."

"Okay, then . . . ," Teddy said, trying to sound confident in the face of yet another dreadful-looking obstacle, "how do we get around this thing?"

"We don't," Lawrence answered. "That would take too long."

"So what do we do?"

Lawrence pointed at the dark hole. "We go under."

"What?" Teddy exclaimed. "No way! We don't even know what's under there. Do you know how creepy the last place I got trapped was?"

"Come on. It's not getting any less creepy while we wait."

Teddy eyed the crawl space suspiciously. After the claustrophobia of the chimney, crawling into a dark hole with a dead kid was the last thing he wanted to do. On the other hand, Lawrence had almost told a joke. *My guide is perking up*, Teddy thought. And besides, he had no choice.

Lawrence went first—otherwise Teddy might not have been able to make himself go in at all. He pulled out his flashlight and shined it ahead as they squeezed through the opening and began to belly-crawl like army commandoes.

The low ceiling was a rat's nest of tangled roots, and

Teddy's backpack snagged on it almost immediately. It slid off as though the roots overhead were trying to rip it away from him. He rolled over and caught it by one strap, wrestling it back.

"Hurry up," Lawrence called back to him.

"Coming," Teddy said, pushing his pack in front of him along the ground.

They hadn't gone far when the flashlight beam illuminated a dark, furry lump—some kind of animal. It appeared to be sleeping. Lawrence crawled over to it.

"Don't wake it up, whatever it is," Teddy whispered.

"It's a dog," Lawrence said.

"Some sort of rabid, monster attack dog?"

"No. Just a dog."

Teddy eased forward to join him. It *was* a normal dog—an Australian cattle dog, from the look of it. It didn't move.

"Sleeping?" Teddy said hopefully.

"Dead," Lawrence replied. "This is Joey's dog."

Teddy had heard of animals crawling into dark places to die, but the dog looked young and, with the exception of being dead, perfectly healthy.

"Look here," Lawrence said. He pointed to the dog's

face, which was curled in a permanent grimace. Tiny bloodstains trailed from two small holes in the dog's snout. "What do you suppose those wounds are?"

"Don't know," Teddy said. "And not sure I want to. How much farther?"

"Don't know."

"I think we should get going, and—"

Teddy froze mid-sentence, interrupted by a rattling sound, like a maraca shaken too fast. It was recognizable even to a boy who wasn't from the desert, and it chilled him to the bone.

CHAPTER 29

Teddy flicked the flashlight beam up. The rattlesnake was coiled less than a foot from him, its thin tongue licking the air. Its beehive-shaped rattle rose behind it, vibrating back and forth.

Lawrence lay on his belly, still as a stone.

"Don't move," Teddy breathed—if they even twitched, it would strike Lawrence, who was closer. It occurred to Teddy that if the rattler got Lawrence, he would be rid of the boy taking him to the tree. But it didn't seem right.

Teddy was still holding his backpack in front of him, and an idea occurred to him. He shoved the pack suddenly with both arms, flinging it between the rattler and Lawrence.

The snake struck, and its fangs sank into the thick fabric on the inside of the pack's open pocket. Before the snake could shake loose, Teddy leaped on his backpack. He pinned the squirming reptile underneath. The rattler coiled angrily, twisting most of its long body into the pocket to join its trapped head. Teddy grabbed its tail, stuffing it in behind the body, then he yanked the zipper closed.

With the snake contained, Teddy rolled onto his back and shuddered, wiping sweat from his brow. "It's more scared of you than you are of it," Teddy explained to Lawrence, panting.

"I wasn't scared," Lawrence said. "It can't kill *me*."

"What?" Teddy exclaimed. "You were never in any danger?"

Lawrence nodded. "Right. It's Joey's death, not mine. But be careful—I figure everything here can kill *you*. And if I don't get you to the tree in one piece, it might drain me instead. I ain't got much life left."

Lawrence sounded stern, and it seemed to Teddy like he was speaking loudly on purpose, trying to be overheard. But then his rigid face softened for a moment, and he whispered, "But, hey, thanks anyway for trying to save me."

CHAPTER 30

They crawled on their bellies for several more minutes, until Lawrence pushed a tangle of roots apart. Dust blew in, which told Teddy they'd found an exit. Lawrence scooted between the roots, and Teddy saw him stand up on the other side. They were through.

Teddy slid out of the crawl space and joined him. It was still dusty outside, but the wind was weakening, and there was less sand flying around. Teddy guessed they were approaching the calm eye of the storm—which meant they were getting close to the tree.

He decided that when they finally broke through the dust and wind, he would simply sprint for the house. Despite the hints of emotion he'd prompted in Lawrence, the tall boy still had the energy of a slug. Teddy was sure he could outrun him. Walter and Albert were out of the picture. If he was able to dodge Sloot, Joey, and Oliver, he could make a break for the window and climb back into his own world.

As they continued on, the dust thinned, and the sycamore rose in front of them. It lorded over the darkness, more dominant here in the world it had created than in the light of day. Despite its trunk being still more than thirty yards away, its twisting branches reached over the boys' heads and into the storm beyond them.

Teddy didn't sprint toward it. Instead, he froze, suddenly drained of courage. He glanced at Lawrence, who wore the same expression he'd shown when Teddy first saw him—none.

"Are you going to make a run for it?" Lawrence asked.

Teddy was surprised that the boy knew exactly what he planned to do. "I *was*," he said.

"No one's stopping you," Lawrence said.

"Really?"

"I brought you this far," the tall boy replied, glancing up at the branches as if to make sure they weren't listening. "And I'll need to chase you when you go. Understand?"

Teddy nodded in agreement. Lawrence nodded back, then he bent down to tie his shoe, lowering his head and turning his eyes away from Teddy.

It was now or never, Teddy thought, and he took off running toward the house.

Lawrence waited a moment before he looked up. "Hey!" he shouted halfheartedly. "Come back here!" He rose and stumbled, tripping over his untied shoelace.

The tree groaned and rotated its huge limbs toward Teddy as he broke out of the waning storm and into the open. The A-house was visible beneath the sycamore on the other side of the trunk, and Teddy headed straight for it.

Teddy heard a whistling sound above him and dodged to his right just as a giant branch whizzed past and slammed into the ground where he had been only a moment earlier. He leaped over another limb and danced through a tangle of roots that wove up through the sand. The tree was a split-second slower than him, and as Teddy neared the A-house, he almost dared to hope that he would reach it.

But then he saw Sloot step out from behind the trunk, flanked by Joey and Oliver.

CHAPTER 31

Teddy trotted to a stop between the tree and the house, facing the dead boys. He was trying to remain calm so that he wouldn't miss a chance to get past them, but he couldn't help his anger.

"You brought me here!" he accused.

"Aww, you're not sore at us, are you?" Sloot said. "We're your friends."

"No you're not," Teddy said. "You're the one who tried to get me into the tree."

"Sloot told me to hide in the chimney," Oliver offered innocently.

"Shut up, Olive Oyl," Sloot snapped, "or I'll bust you in the chops."

"Don't call me that," Oliver complained.

By now, Lawrence had trotted to a stop behind Teddy and stood over him like a reluctant prison guard. Teddy cursed himself for taking too long to get to the house.

"You were the first one in," Teddy said, pointing directly at Sloot. "You helped lure everyone else."

Teddy's accusation drew a smirk from Sloot. "You think I'm bad?"

"I think you're scared," Teddy said.

That quieted Sloot, and he stared off into the distance, a reaction Teddy hadn't expected. The sycamore groaned impatiently above them, and Teddy braced himself for an attack, watching for low-hanging branches in the darkness above.

"Have you tried to fight back?" Teddy asked. "Tried to escape?"

Sloot spoke without looking at Teddy. "My dad used to take his boots off in our yard when he came home from a hard day at the nuke-u-lar plant. He'd empty the sand out of them right beneath the old sycamore. Sometimes he would get mad at me, but I could always climb faster than he could throw a boot—"

"I mean escape from the *tree*," Teddy interrupted.

Sloot looked up at him, his eyes glistening with tears that wouldn't quite come. "The tree is where I came *to* escape."

"Well, I'm not staying here," Teddy said. "I got into this world on my own, and I'm going right back out!" Teddy marched past them to the bedroom window in the house. He was surprised when they didn't try to stop him.

Teddy pushed up on the window frame. It didn't budge. His heart sank as he turned to find Sloot grinning.

"You dumb palooka." Sloot laughed. "It's locked." He waved to Lawrence, Oliver, and Joey. "Take him to the tree," he commanded, "before it sucks one of the rest of us completely dry instead."

CHAPTER 32

The dead boys converged on Teddy, and he had to think fast. He whipped out the flashlight and shined it straight into Oliver's eyes. Oliver doubled over, and Teddy shoved him to the ground. It bought Teddy just enough time to yank the zipper open on his backpack.

"Get in there!" Sloot yelled at Lawrence. He pointed wildly at the scuffle between Teddy and the other boys.

Joey was on Teddy next, his hands grabbing at Teddy's shirt. They struggled, standing toe-to-toe for a moment before Teddy pulled the pocket of the backpack wide. Joey looked down just in time to see the rattlesnake's triangular head dart out and sink its fangs into his leg.

The dead boy winced as the snake dropped to the ground and slithered through his legs off into the desert. It left behind two small holes in Joey's flesh, a pinpoint of blood leaking from each one.

Joey looked up at Teddy with pleading eyes, but Teddy couldn't help him. Joey staggered backward. The other boys stared at him, forgetting Teddy for a moment as Joey died in front of them. Shock and poison worked together, dropping Joey facedown into the sand, and it was over in moments.

Teddy didn't wait for the others to recover. If the bedroom window was locked, there was always the broken attic window on the roof. He ran for the porch, hoping to climb up one of its pillars before the kids could catch him.

Halfway to the house, Oliver intercepted Teddy with a flying tackle, and they both went down in a heap. As Oliver wrestled to keep Teddy on the ground, Sloot sauntered over and cocked his foot back to deliver a vicious kick to Teddy's head.

Teddy braced himself for impact. But then Lawrence

grabbed Sloot by the collar and hoisted him up off of his feet. There was still no emotion in Lawrence's face that Teddy could see, but the force with which he rammed Sloot headfirst into the wall of the A-house seemed a bit more than necessary.

Oliver rolled off of Teddy to see what had happened and found Lawrence's foot suddenly in the middle of his chest.

"Get up," Lawrence said to Teddy. "And stay down," he said to Oliver, holding him on the ground with his weight.

Teddy didn't hesitate. He hopped to his feet, climbed onto the porch, and began to shimmy up a pillar. The tree was moving overhead, but its lower branches were too thick and slow—it couldn't bend them fast enough to stop him.

Lawrence helped push Teddy up, standing on Oliver's chest for a few extra inches of height, and Teddy grabbed hold of the gutter that ran along the edge of the porch roof. He swung one leg over the edge and wriggled his body up onto the rooftop. Tree limbs swung in to sweep him off, but he rolled and dodged them, clambering up the roof toward the broken window.

Teddy was almost to the window when he heard a shout of alarm behind him. He turned around to see Lawrence rising up into the air, lifted by a branch that had curled about his waist. Leaves quickly covered his exposed skin, beginning to feed.

Teddy stared, helpless, as the tree drained the last of Lawrence's spirit. It happened very fast—there was not much of Lawrence left. The tall boy writhed in the tree's grasp, the remaining color in his face fading. Then he gave one last shudder and went still.

CHAPTER 33

The tree continued to suck at Lawrence's motionless form, his body caving in wherever the leaves touched him. As Teddy watched in horror, Lawrence's body began to disintegrate into powder, and the dust of his remains drifted away on the wind. In a matter of minutes, he'd disappeared completely.

Below, Oliver and Joey marveled wide-eyed and horrified at the fate of their former companion. By this time, Sloot had gotten up, and he glared at the other boys, jabbing his finger at the tree.

"You see? You see?" he cried. "That's what you get!"

The tree shook as though renewed by the last bit of energy it had drained from Lawrence. Its branches turned their attention back to Teddy. They were suddenly more nimble, and a narrow limb darted after him, whipping around his leg.

Teddy yanked the hatchet from his pack and brought it down with the force of desperation, chopping the branch in two. The severed end released his leg and writhed on the roof, oozing black sap. He looked up just in time to avoid a larger branch hurtling toward him by throwing himself flat on the roof as it whistled over his head.

He saw two more following close behind. But he also saw the window was within reach. Gathering his legs beneath him, Teddy launched himself through the opening in the broken glass.

He landed hard on the attic's beams but scrambled up and hurriedly started making his way through the room. He stepped over and ducked under the tangles of tree branches that curled around the rafters and wove through the floor beams, balancing carefully.

It seemed as though the limbs had grown and expanded to fill the space, and Teddy was thankful they were so entwined they couldn't move to grab him. When he was halfway across the attic, he swung the flashlight toward the trapdoor. There he saw a dark lump the size of a person wedged between the narrow floor beams. As he approached, he realized that the lump was a boy curled up in a fetal position.

The boy was breathing, but seemed to be asleep. He looked about the same size and weight as Teddy himself. Unfortunately, he was positioned directly atop the trapdoor so that Teddy would have to move him to get the door open and return to his own world.

But if I can wrestle him out of the way, he thought, *I'm free!*

Teddy grabbed the boy's body and shoved him off of the trapdoor. As the boy rolled over, he stared up at Teddy with glazed eyes. Teddy's heart leaped into his throat as he instantly recognized the face.

Oh no, he thought. *It's me!*

CHAPTER 34

Teddy stared in horror at his own motionless body. There was a long gash in his leg, and his shorts were completely red. It looked like he'd already lost a lot of blood. The end of the sharp branch that had cut him was still buried in the wound, sucking out his life like a straw.

This is my place, Teddy thought.

He knew instantly that he had to get himself out of the house or he'd die in this secret place and never be found, just like the other boys. He reached down and pulled the parasite branch from his torn flesh with a sickening *pop*. It squirmed against his grip, trying to worm its way back into his unconscious body, but Teddy wrestled it aside and pulled out his hatchet again. He gave it a firm chop, and the dismembered branch fell between the floor beams.

Heaving his own limp body up onto his back in a fireman's carry, Teddy turned to discover that the previously still attic branches had come alive and were weaving a wall between him and the broken window. The tree wanted him to stay.

But Teddy snarled, angry. He lowered his body onto the floor beams, stomped across the attic, and met the tangle of branches head-on. They blocked the window, but he swung the hatchet hard and severed two small limbs, spattering the beams with black, sappy fluid. His backswing caught a larger branch and cut it almost in half. It flopped like a beheaded snake, and the other limbs shrank from the weapon, clearing a path to the window.

Teddy hauled his body back up and dragged himself out through the broken glass.

Together, they tumbled down the slanted roof, out of control. The hatchet went flying as Teddy scrambled for a handhold.

He caught the edge of the rain gutter, but it gave way, sending him down to the ground. Still, his grip on the gutter slowed his fall just enough that he hit without feeling any bones snap.

Then his own body fell right on top of him.

CHAPTER 35

The impact knocked him over, but Teddy quickly rolled to his feet. He looked for his body, but he didn't see it anywhere. He took a step and felt a vicious sting in his leg—the cut from the branch was now on his own thigh. Teddy pressed a hand to the wound and scanned the immediate area, but there was only one of him.

I reunited with my body, he realized.

The physical wound hurt, but without the sharp end of the branch jabbed into his leg, it wasn't bleeding anymore. Teddy almost collapsed with relief. He was no longer dying.

But he was still trapped in the dim world, body and soul together. And the A-house was not a way out—it was meant to be his tomb, so Teddy knew he would never go back inside. Even if he'd wanted to, he wouldn't have the chance. The tree stood directly over him like an executioner in the barren darkness.

"There's no escape," Sloot called. He stood a safe distance away from Teddy, still rubbing his head where Lawrence had slammed him into the wall.

Oliver stood behind him. "Anywhere you go, there it is," he added.

Teddy balanced unsteadily on his injured leg and faced the two dead boys. "Well, you can tell that stupid, ugly, moldy thing to go rot."

"Tell it yourself," Sloot said.

A huge branch swooped down and buffeted Teddy from behind. He flew forward and landed facedown on the desert floor. But Teddy didn't stay down. He defiantly crawled back to his feet to face the monstrous tree.

"You're just a huge bully!" he yelled, spitting sand. "And I eat bullies for breakfast!"

He pulled the small flashlight and shined it up into the

low branches. It wasn't much, but they squirmed under its light, parting to reveal Albert, the tree's next victim.

Teddy clenched his fist in rage—the tree was sucking the other boys dry, because it couldn't get him. He kept the light trained on the leaves, which were pasted all over Albert's body. They peeled themselves loose, shrinking away from the light until Albert dangled by a single branch, then dropped.

Albert landed in the sand at Teddy's feet. He was alive, but barely, his energy drained so low that he could not even lift his own neck. Teddy bent down and cradled Albert in his lap.

"I'm sorry," Albert moaned through dry, cracked lips. "At first I did try to bring you here, but then you were nice to me, and I wished I hadn't. Now you're stuck, and it's all my fault."

"I'm still your friend," Teddy whispered to Albert, who stared up at him with eyes full of grateful tears.

But then Albert's eyes went wide, and Teddy turned just in time to see the branch that had struck him before swinging around again, this time whipping toward his head. Just in time, Teddy ducked down and met the branch with the flashlight beam.

The limb swung close enough to the flashlight bulb that it caught the brightest part of the beam. The light cut into the branch with a sizzling sound, leaving a shallow black scar three inches wide. The branch retreated, and the entire tree spasmed as though in pain, shaking the ground.

Teddy seized the chance to haul Albert up to his feet, but almost immediately, more branches began to descend. As thick as elephants' legs, they bent to the ground around the boys, blocking any path of escape. At the same time, thinner limbs snaked straight down toward them like hanging vines to grab them.

"Back to back!" Teddy snapped, leaning up against Albert so that they could see both directions. He'd hurt the tree with the flashlight, and it gave him hope that they could fight it. Teddy dumped the last of his supplies from his pack, desperate for anything else that could help them. All that was left were the crowbar, the spray bottle, and the rope. He grabbed the rope and crowbar for himself and handed the flashlight and bottle to Albert.

"What's this?" Albert asked.

"Weed killer," Teddy said, then the pack of narrow limbs snatched both boys off their feet.

CHAPTER 36

Teddy was tossed upward by the branches on a dizzying trip through the darkness, much faster than when Sloot first invited him into the tree for a view. Higher and higher he was passed, until he could no longer see the ground. In no time, he had lost track of Albert, who was being handled by other branches.

The limbs were not gentle with Teddy, but they moved him with enough care that he decided the tree was not planning to kill him yet. He noticed that the branches were growing thinner as they traded him from one to the next, and Teddy realized that he was nearing the treetop.

With a jolt, the last few branches halted his ascent, and he teetered in the dimness at the top of the tree. It was as if the tree was holding him up like a prize before draining him of his life.

But Teddy didn't wait for the leaves to latch on to him. Ever since he'd realized the tree was going to take him, his hand had been wrapped around the climbing rope. He slid one end through two of his belt loops and the other end around the treetop, where he tied a hurried knot.

He saw Albert about fifteen feet below him, also clinging to the trunk. He'd gotten loose from his branches and was holding the parasitic leaves at bay by burning them with the beam of the small flashlight and squirting them with weed killer, which made them curl and crumple.

For a moment, Teddy grinned, proud of Albert for fighting back, then he wrenched himself free of the small upper branches still holding him and fell.

He plunged downward for a dizzying moment before his rope caught and swung him into the trunk, where he fended off the impact with his feet. The branches tried to chase him, but the thicker limbs had trouble bending inward to grab him, and he swung the crowbar, smacking the smaller branches hard, cracking them or tearing off leaves with every blow.

By this time, Albert had wedged himself between the trunk and the base of a heavy branch. Teddy climbed back up a few feet and joined him.

"Now what?" Albert said.

Teddy didn't exactly know *what*, but his first thought was that they should get out of the tree. "We can climb down near the trunk where the branches can't bend easily to reach us."

"It won't matter, Albert said. "They'll crush us when we reach the ground. Even if we get away, it will always find us."

More branches were bending in their direction now, both from above and below, all straining to get at them. Teddy realized that many were too big to be beaten away with the crowbar.

"My hatchet is down there somewhere, and we can try to get Walter's saw," Teddy suggested. "We'll cut the tree down!"

"No way." Albert shook his head. "Its trunk is twenty feet wide, and its roots are everywhere—"

Just then, Albert went silent, horrified. He pointed past Teddy at the pitch-black, four-foot hole that gaped in the trunk of the tree directly behind him.

"The mouth!" Teddy gasped.

CHAPTER 37

Around the great cavity in the tree the bark was split and cracked with age, and its rolled edges glistened with oozing black sap. The deep darkness inside hid all else. Teddy hung helpless before it, suspended by the rope.

"It's not a mouth," Albert whispered. "No teeth, no tongue."

"Hand me the flashlight," Teddy breathed, too scared to speak any louder.

Albert passed it up. "Do you want the weed killer?"

Teddy grabbed the flashlight and took the spray bottle too, for good measure. "I'm just going to have a look."

He shined the beam into the hole, revealing a leering face that stared straight back at him. It was Sloot. The angry boy burst from the darkness and grabbed Teddy by the throat.

"This is my place!" he yelled. "Mine! Find your own place to die!"

Teddy swung away from the trunk to escape, but Sloot came with him, one hand on Teddy's neck, the other wrapped around his waist. It was all Teddy could do to keep hold of the rope so their combined weight didn't rip his belt loops off and send them tumbling to the ground.

As they swung together on the rope, Teddy felt himself fading, losing strength to fight back or hold on—the constant attacks were finally taking their toll. But as he gasped for breaths that wouldn't come, he heard Albert shout, "Get off my friend!"

Then, miraculously, Teddy was free. Beneath him, Albert and Sloot plummeted through the tree, smacking against branches as they fell. Teddy realized that his chubby friend had jumped from the safety of his branch to tear Sloot off of him.

He heard both boys cry out in pain as the tree beat them viciously on the way down, seemingly punishing them for their failure to deliver a new victim. Teddy squeezed his eyes shut as he twirled slowly on the rope; he couldn't watch.

When their grunts and screams had subsided, Teddy opened his eyes. He was hanging directly in front of the hole again. He didn't have the strength to climb or the nerve to drop, and so he simply peered inside.

He was surprised to see vague images in the darkness that grew clearer the longer he stared—a distant moonlit river, rows of split-level homes, and the empty desert beyond. Clearest of all was Officer Barnes standing below, leaning against the trunk of the oversized sycamore.

The scene became familiar and vivid, not nightmarish and dust-blurred like the exaggerated world of the tree. And Teddy remembered that this was one of the ways the sycamore had tried to bring him *into* the world.

It's not a mouth, he realized. *It's a door!*

With this thought, he found his strength, and Teddy set his feet against a branch to launch himself into the hole. But he was still tied to the tree above, and there wasn't enough rope for him to fully enter the yawning darkness. He held the dripping rim of the opening and felt desperately in his pocket for Mulligan's knife.

It was still there, so Teddy pulled it out to slash at the rope. At the same time, two massive branches bent in his direction, straining against their own rigidity. They zeroed in on him, like thirty-foot hammers coming down on a nail.

Teddy sawed madly at the rope with the last of his strength. As it finally gave way, the monstrous sycamore gave a high-pitched squeal and Teddy plunged into the hollow of the screaming tree.

CHAPTER 38

Through the hole in the sycamore Teddy fell, tumbling from branch to branch in the clear, moonlit night. The branches did not let him down gently this time. Instead, they bashed and pounded him as though he was a piñata.

Just when Teddy thought the branches would beat him to death, he dropped free of the tree. He fell unhindered for a moment, then Officer Barnes was there, positioned below to break Teddy's fall. Teddy plowed into the policeman's arms and chest, and they both sprawled out on the ground from the impact.

Teddy's cheeks stung where they'd been whipped by

small branches, his left arm hurt badly after hitting a thicker limb, and the wound in his leg had been torn open again. There would be dozens of bruises too, in various places. But more than anything, he was exhausted. He looked up at Barnes, who was kneeling over him, and murmured, "Thank you." Then he closed his eyes and let himself fade into unconsciousness.

. . .

"You're awake," Barnes said as Teddy opened his eyes to daylight streaming in through his hospital window. "And I have good news and bad news."

Teddy turned his head to find the familiar cop sitting in a chair beside his adjustable bed with several empty coffee cups beside him. It was clear he'd been waiting there for hours.

"You're going to be okay." Barnes continued. "That's the good news. We got you some first aid for that nasty cut on your leg, some fluids for your dehydration—which was a bit strange—and that sprained arm isn't broken. You can leave anytime. The bad news is that your next stop is the police station to talk about breaking into that abandoned house, among other things."

"I know where they are," Teddy said.

"Who?"

"The dead boys. I found them."

"Teddy, from the blood we discovered in the attic, I think all you *found* was a sharp stick. You passed out from loss of blood. Somehow you recovered enough to drag yourself out the attic window and fall through the tree. You're just lucky your mom woke up and called me to report you missing. I was just walking around the house's yard when I heard you bouncing through the branches."

Teddy shook his head. Barnes had it all wrong.

"And after you fell, this is what *I found*," Barnes continued, holding up Henry Mulligan's knife.

Teddy shifted uncomfortably in the hospital bed. "Am I going to jail?" He asked.

Barnes opened his notebook and clicked out his pen. "Did you do it?"

Teddy slumped into his pillow. He nodded, mumbling "yes," and Barnes wrote it down.

Two hours later, Teddy was riding through the center of Richland in a police cruiser for the second time in three days. Being alive was some consolation, but now he'd be going to juvenile hall. There would probably be rough kids there, he thought, but at least they wouldn't be dead.

As they passed Malley's Pharmacy, he looked out the window at a row of boxy homes that all looked alike and an old church with a huge, crumbling chimney.

"Stop!" Teddy yelled suddenly. "That's it!"

Barnes pulled over. "What? What's wrong?"

"That's where Oliver went."

"Oliver who?"

"Oliver Strand."

"The boy who disappeared in 2000?" Barnes asked.

"Do me this one favor," Teddy begged. "Remember all the stuff I knew about Albert and Walter?"

"Yes."

"Please. I'll tell you exactly why I went into Mr. Mulligan's trailer and the A-house if you just come inside with me for a minute."

"Okay, Teddy." Barnes sighed. "One minute."

Inside the church, Teddy immediately recognized the

huge brick fireplace. His heart began to pound again.

"I'm indulging you here, Teddy," Barnes said. The officer got down on his back and scooted into the fireplace, shining his flashlight up the chimney. "Personally, I think this is ridicu—"

There was a moment of silence as Teddy waited for Barnes to finish grumbling. But suddenly the officer cried out instead, "Teddy, I need your help!"

"What?"

"There's a boy stuck in the chimney!"

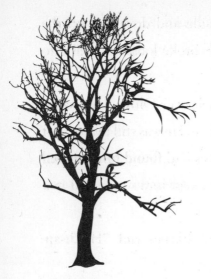

CHAPTER 39

The next few minutes were a blur. Barnes was shouting orders and thrusting the flashlight into Teddy's hands. The frantic officer rushed down the hall with the pastor to call an ambulance and find hedge shears.

While he waited, Teddy stuck his head into the fire-place and shone the flashlight up. He could just make out a pair of feet dangling about five feet above him. He could also see a maze of old tree roots that had grown through the broken chimney and were wrapped around the legs.

Then Barnes pushed him aside and dove in with the shears. Moments later, the body broke loose and fell into the open fireplace.

Teddy watched as Barnes knelt over Oliver. He looked pale and weak, but impossibly alive. He was still twelve, just as he'd been when the tree's roots had found him trapped in the chimney a decade ago and kept him suspended in a perverse half-life.

"This can't be Oliver Strand," Barnes said. "He disappeared ten years ago."

"It can't be," Teddy said, "but it is. And we shouldn't stay here very long, because I know where the rest are too."

Once the ambulance arrived, Barnes and Teddy left Oliver to the medics with as little explanation as possible and quickly climbed back into the patrol car.

They raced through the streets of Richland. This time, Teddy sat in the front seat, holding the borrowed shears on his lap.

"There!" Teddy pointed to a house on Catskill Street with a crawl space underneath. "Tell them to bring rattler antivenom." Barnes no longer questioned him, and when more medics arrived to attend to a groggy Joey, he and Teddy took off in his patrol car again, this time headed for Lynwood Court.

Emergency crews Barnes had called on his radio were already digging like mad, and within minutes they recovered Walter from the ground between the houses where the sewer trench had been installed forty years earlier. When he came up, he was filthy, stinky, and spitting dirt, but very much alive.

"Hey, Scaredy," Walter whispered, choking out mouthful of sand and a gritty chuckle.

At the river, Barnes put a hand on Teddy's shoulder as they watched the police divers Barnes had called plunge into the water.

"It's been thirty years." Barnes said. "The water will have washed Albert away."

"The others made it," Teddy said, though he had the same worry.

Moments later, a police diver floated up with Albert in his arms. As soon as the chubby boy hit the air, Teddy heard him take a gasping breath.

Teddy rushed to the water's edge to meet him as they dragged him ashore.

Albert looked up and him, wet and weary, and mustered a smile that made his eyes squinch up. "I told you I wasn't totally dead," he said weakly.

"Hey, man, thanks for saving me in there," Teddy said.

"Are you kidding?" Albert chuckled. "Of course. I'm your friend, right?"

Before Teddy could answer, the medics rushed in and whisked Albert away.

They hurried out into the desert next. Teddy was excited to talk to Lawrence, to celebrate their escape, and to thank the tall boy for helping him.

Two hours later, they found him under a layer of desert sand in his ditch. He was lying on his side, still curled up against the dust storm from fifty years ago. But the roots that once held him had dried out and retreated, no longer interested in Lawrence for energy.

Teddy sat down beside him, and the rest of the search party stepped away to give him a private moment.

"I want to thank you for helping me," Teddy said at

length as he stared out over the desert. Lawrence had made it to within one hundred yards of the gas station at the end of Saint Street before he'd given up. "You were right. This is a lonely place."

Teddy got no answer. Lawrence's body had been scoured by the wind and sand, and all that was left was polished white bone. There was no life in him anymore.

If only Lawrence had known how close he was, Teddy thought. *If only Sloot hadn't encouraged him to lie down and rest. If only the tree hadn't sucked him completely dry.*

Sloot was the final piece of the puzzle, but Teddy had a pretty good idea of where he was. Within half an hour, they were back at the tree. On the way over, Barnes had called in a tree trimmer, and now Teddy stood with him in the bucket of a mechanical lift as it rose toward the tree's giant knothole.

When they got close enough, they both saw him.

Sloot was sitting inside the hole, his back propped against the inner wall, knees drawn up to his chest. A rotted baseball cap sat atop his head. He was emaciated, a mere shell of the boy he'd been on the other side. There were no roots or branches wrapped around him. Instead, his back, arms, and legs had fused with the wood—he was being absorbed directly into the heart of the tree.

As Teddy and Barnes both starred in horror, Sloot's body twitched.

"It's draining him right now!" Teddy exclaimed. "He's dying!"

Barnes leaned out of the bucket, but he couldn't maneuver his large body into the hole to make a grab for Sloot. "I can't reach!" he said.

Teddy gritted his teeth. "I'll try."

Barnes held Teddy's legs while he leaned out of the bucket to grab Sloot. He was halfway into the hole when he felt the edges of the opening clamping down on his chest.

"Look out!" Barnes cried in disbelief. "It's closing!"

As Teddy made a desperate grab for Sloot's hand, Sloot opened his eyes. He spoke in a low, leafy voice that was an echo of the tree's own groans in the wind.

"You're back."

"No, I'm not back," Teddy said. "I'm out. Come with me."

Sloot's body continued to melt into the wood—it was getting tough to tell where the tree ended and Sloot began. His mouth spread into a hideous grin.

"No. You come in here with me, pal."

Suddenly, Sloot reached out and grabbed Teddy's wrist with a twisted, wooden hand. Teddy fought to free himself from its grip as the edges of the hole pressed tighter on his chest. He saw he could not free Sloot—the tree had him, and it would have Teddy too if he stayed.

"I'm stronger than you," Teddy said, as much to the tree as to the boy, and he wrenched his wrist from Sloot's weakening hold on him.

Just then, Barnes yanked Teddy out of the tree's mouth, and he flopped back into the lift's bucket. The hole squeezed closed behind him, narrowing until it was just a puckered knot in the wood.

"Down!" Teddy shouted, his voice shaking.

"Okay," Barnes said.

Barnes jerked the lift lever, and the bucket rocked backward, moving safely away from the hole. "We don't need to come back," he said, "do we?"

"No," Teddy confirmed. "He's gone."

EPILOGUE

Days later, Teddy awoke in his own room, amazed and delighted to find that he'd finally had a full night's sleep and that there was nothing any scarier to greet him than his fawning mother. He wolfed down the breakfast she'd made him and headed outside.

The police cruiser pulled up right on time, and Officer Barnes stepped out onto the sidewalk dressed in coveralls and leather gloves. Teddy limped down the walk to the patrol car. He still ached all over, especially where the tree had stabbed him. He wondered if that wound would ever completely heal.

"Morning, Teddy," Barnes called. "How are you feeling?"

"Fabulous," Teddy joked, rubbing his thigh. "How are the others?"

Barnes lowered his voice. "Okay, but they're under observation at the hospital," he said. "Nobody's been told except their families. Understandably, they're very excited and very confused."

"I'll bet," Teddy agreed, then he glanced over at the sycamore tree. The tree was still tall and imposing, but its leaves had yellowed and wilted. Teddy was no longer drawn to it, nor terrified of it, he discovered. "Well, let's get on with it."

"Great," Barnes chirped. "I was worried you might be a little too overwhelmed by everything to go through with this so soon. You sure you're ready?"

Teddy nodded. "Ready as I'll ever be, I guess."

Barnes handed him a pair of gloves, goggles, and a hard hat. "Good," he said, "because I've got a crew with chainsaws waiting."

They strode across the A-house lawn, where Barnes signaled to a man standing beneath the sycamore with the biggest chainsaw Teddy had ever seen. He pulled the cord, and the saw roared to life.

Teddy stood a safe distance away and watched, anticipating that the tree would be unnaturally tough and resist the chainsaw's teeth. But when the buzzing saw dug into the bark, it didn't grind against hard wood. Instead, dust flew in a cloud, and the trunk came apart in great, dry chunks.

"It's all coming down!" the man yelled, and he turned to run away.

The massive sycamore shuddered and swayed, but it

didn't topple sideways, like a normal tree. Instead, it simply collapsed, falling straight down in on itself. And as the trunk and huge branches struck the ground, they disintegrated into powder, which rose in a cloud to obscure the entire A-house.

Teddy waited beside Barnes, wide-eyed and half expecting the tree's roots to crawl out of the maelstrom after him. But when the cloud cleared, there was nothing left but a pile of dust on the lawn.

"It was rotten to the core the whole time," Barnes said.

"No," Teddy corrected him. "It was starving."

At that moment, a gigantic flock of seagulls from the river swooped in. They passed over the A-house, then rose into the sky like a single ghostly-white sheet. It was magnificent, and Teddy smiled for the first time he could remember in days. He couldn't wait to tell Albert.